GYPSIES

Children's poem.

My Mother said, I never should
Play with the gypsies in the wood.
If I did, she would say;
'Naughty girl to disobay!

Your hair shan't curl, and your shoes shan't shine,
you gypsy girl, you shan't be mine!
And my father said, that if I did,
He'd rap my head with the teapot lid.

Author Anonymous.

-

'I must have been a very very bad girl!'

Its funny really. When you think about the kind of guy you are going to marry, a Romany living in an old caravan does not normally come to mind!

Can't think why, can you?!

So, there I was. 19 years old and fed up with 'normal' guys who only wanted one thing. Yep you guessed it!

But then....

along comes this guy,

tall, skinny, bad hair, ugly/handsome.....

did I say bad hair? Oh yes!

And that was just the beginning!
But little did I know that he was a gypsy!

Oh boy!
Gypsies and gorgi's don't mix.....do they?
I was about to find out!

-

Honest, raw, colourful, and downright hilarious!

Definition.

Gorgi, gorgio, gorgia, gorgie, gorji -Non gypsy.

Romany gypsy- originated from India, travelled through Egypt and settled in Britain and Europe.

Irish Travellers – Came from Ireland centuries ago. Some chose to leave their houses and take to the road, others worked for Romany's and took up the lifestyle.

Pikey or Diddikai – A derogatory word (s) for mixed race of gypsy and gorgi, or gypsy and other.

-

All named photos are my own.
+ Public Domain photos, Google Images.

-

Photo list:

Janey and Alby.

Gina Loveridge and Dinah.

Dennis Loveridge.

Jake Loveridge.

Loveridge Family.

Nell Rose Loveridge.

Dedicated To

Jeff (Jake) who I could never imagine living without. I mean, who else can make me laugh till I cry?

My son Daniel, who is my pride and joy.

And the wonderful Gypsy and traveller people who get a bad press purely because they aren't given a chance to shine.

Not forgetting my best friend Les who said I could do it.
Miss you.

-

Copyright © 2017

by Nell Rose Loveridge.

All rights reserved. This book or any portion thereof may not be reproduced or used in any manner whatsoever without the express written permission of the publisher except for the use of brief quotations in a book review.

Printed in the UK by Amazon Kindle

direct publishing.

GYPSIES.

Nell Rose Loveridge.

Chapter 1

I ran away with a Gypsy!
My parents raised me to be the product of a normal working class household.
Ouch! They freaked out big time!

I mean lets face it, your Mum and Dad expect their 'beautiful daughter' to marry someone special.
Like a solicitor, or maybe even a doctor.

A doctor in the family? Yep that would be perfect.
Mum would have been on the phone to him every single second of the day asking him all sorts of questions such as; 'So you think this prescription is good for piles?' or 'Tell me doctor, is baby cream good for warts?'
But when she found out that I was going to marry a gypsy she screamed;
'WHAT THE BLOODY HELL DO YOU THINK YOU'RE DOING? MARRY A GYPSY? WHAT? HAVE YOU GONE MAD?'
Oh crap cakes, now I was for it!
Taking a huge breath she yelled at dad, 'Jim, talk to her, for Gods sake!'
But my dad just smiled.

Then he laughed. Then it was a huge guffaw that split his face wide open with a grin.

'Oh Ena leave her alone, he's probably very nice.'

He took my hand.

'She knows what she's doing.' he said.

That's my dad, gives everybody a chance until proven wrong. My mum on the other hand, wasn't so polite.

'He looks like a typical Romany,' she hissed.

How on earth would she know? How many gypsies has she met in her life?

Oh yes, one!

Ironically she was very friendly with old Rose who she spoke to once a week at the shop.
So that was okay!

As for Jake, I don't know whether she was insulting him or just being very observant!

Yes he was a Gypsy, or Romany as they prefer to be called. Spot on Ma!

Suddenly I remembered the quote from when I was a kid.

'If you don't behave I'll give you to the gypsies!'

My head started thumping, and sweat beaded between my breasts.

Boy was I nervous! My mum was so old fashioned it was beyond belief!

Then a thought popped into my head.

Marry a gypsy? I must have been a very bad girl! I tried not to grin. And got ready for the next assault.

Sniffing, mum glared at me.

'How could you do this to me? He won't ever get a job, you'll end up living in a caravan like....pikies!'

Pikies? She knew the word pikies? Well, who would have guessed?

As you can see, I started to feel a bit sarcastic by this time.

If I opened my mouth I knew I would be in danger of the mud look. Oh sorry, there it was already!

Its that expression all mothers have when they're about to launch into a huge row!

You know the one.

It can turn water into wood. Change calm people into shivering wrecks. And this time, it was aimed at me!

Thinking about it, what gave it away that Jake was a Romany?

Closing my eyes I pictured Jake in front of me.

Um, kind of dreamy!

But to my mum?

'He looks shifty, lazy and a crook!'

Not a good start then!

I was just nineteen years old. I thought I knew it all. The more my mother said no, I said yes.
She said leave him, I went and married him.
Not a good start!
I rubbed one foot against the back of my leg. I tend to do that when I get nervous.
And off we go again.....!

'You only need a horse, pegs and a basket and you will fit in nicely!' followed by a humph.
Then she walked out and slammed the door just to prove a point! But I married him anyway. Oh dear Lord what had I done?

Chapter 2

Neither of us had any money, and much to my mother's shame, we went to live in a Caravan a few miles away.
Yes it was a cliché!
Actually my mother wasn't far wrong.

The site was full of gypsies.

There were a few gorgi's there too. A gorgi, or gorgio is a non gypsy.

I noticed there weren't any old vardo's on the site.

A vardo is what gypsies used to live in before modern caravans appeared.

They were round topped and made of wood. Mainly green or blue, they had patterns around the edges. How families managed to fit everybody in was anybody's guess.

But those times were long gone. This was the 1980's, not 1880.

But some things never changed.

Men sat on their caravan steps. Hammers and knives on their laps, stripping copper wire.

Over in the field at the back of the site, a group of men were burning the metal to remove the plastic covering.

There were piles of different coloured metals scattered around. The bonfire glow warming the air on a frosty day.

Cars and vans were constantly delivering brass and iron to be sorted and the men put it all in boxes to take to the nearby scrap yard.

As I went from car to caravan carrying boxes and various pots and pans, I noticed a woman staring at me from across the road.

I stopped and looked.

Her skin was dark, deep lines etched her face. Her eyes twinkled at me, but the look was wary.

She wore bright coloured clothing. A knee length pleated skirt and huge gold earrings.

I just stared. And she stared back.

I noticed something moving behind me and as I turned round I caught a flash of colour. There, In the neighbours garden, was a large group of women.

Some wore similar attire to the first lady. Others covered their skirts with white aprons.

A few had huge belts over the top of trousers or dresses. And most carried heavy bags which I noticed held knitting and and other mysterious objects.

You have to understand one thing. At this early point in my 'How to be a gypsy for dummies' mental manual I believed all gypsies were secretive 'others' who were sprinkled with fairy dust or something!

Yeah I know, dumb ass!

I noticed that the youngsters wore modern clothes which seemed drab beside their elders.

One thing I did smile at was the earrings! I have never seen so many big bright hoops!

And a lot of the women wore scarves tied around their hair.

The older generation seemed desperate to hold onto their traditions.

The young yearning for the future.

At this point I didn't know whether they would be nice or not.

Turns out that they were really friendly.

But at this point I didn't know what to expect.

Being an outsider, and brainwashed if you like by media and public opinion, I thought that gypsies and travellers were shifty and untrusting.

Well what do you expect? If you get told something long enough then you expect to see it face to face.

I couldn't have been more wrong.

For example after we moved in, there always seemed to be someone knocking on the door with a gift for us.

These presents would either be for the caravan itself, curtains cups and saucers, or personal gifts.

By the time we had unpacked our own belongings, they had brought so much stuff that there was an abundance of bedding, pillows, and even soap and tea!

All this and more, just to make us feel welcome.

I was so surprised.

One woman laughed and said,

'Well girl, you are one of us now!'

This was standard procedure the Gypsy way, I learned later.

I was invited by all the families to come and meet them in their caravans.

Stepping inside one of them I was amazed to see how clean they were. Don't get me wrong, I didn't for one minute think they would be dirty, but I wasn't expecting it to be so scrubbed.

The carpets were bright and clean. All thick pile. The cups and saucers were gold rimmed unlike my old plain ones, and the whole caravan was spotless.

I was afraid to go into their vans because I thought I might dirty their carpet!

'Come on in! Take a seat, don't look so nervous!' laughing, old Ma Smith patted the sofa for me to sit down.

Looking around I perched on the edge of the seat.

'Now if there's anythin' you need asking, then ask it, okay?'

Nothing came to mind, so I just smiled. Looking back I laugh at my naivety.

After a few days I felt right at home.

I also learned a lot from them. How to put up the curtains so that they looked 'quant.'

The best way to pluck a chicken was to lay it in a bowl and pull out the feathers. And so on!

The one time someone came knocking on the door with a brace of rabbits I just looked at Jake and handed them over.

Then I washed my hands and escaped to the shops. I still don't know to this day what happened to those poor bunnies!

Chapter 3

Unlike a lot of the travellers, we were always broke.

But it wasn't through lack of trying.

Jake looked for jobs everywhere and sometimes managed to hold down a job for a few months. But at other times he lost his job and we were back to square one. Then out came the scrap metal.

'How the hell do you do this without cutting your fingers to shreds?' sucking my finger and hopping on one leg I swore under my breath.

'Nah Give it to me you dozy....!' snatching it from my hand, Jake took out a stanley knife and started stripping the wire.

'Right, first of all, hold it in yer hand like this,' he handed it back to me, 'then tie up the other end to the door 'andle, yeah that's right you got it.'

Standing there watching me like a hawk in case I ruined the wire, he went on, 'There's an art to this tottin', make sure you don't.......'

Just as he said don't, I did. Big time! The wire snapped, and I, leaning backwards to get as much pull on it as possible, fell flat on my bum, knife in hand!

'Bloody fucking......!' I scrambled to my feet just as Jake grabbed me by the hand.

'Tell ya what, let me do it, you stupid rackli!' grinning he grabbed the knife and off he went. Expert wire cutter extraordinaire!

'Oh well. One of these days I'll get the hang of it!' I rubbed my sore backside and sat down with a humph.

Let him do it then!

At the end of the day I didn't mind cleaning scrap metal. It was pretty fiddly but copper got a good price at the scrap yard, and even iron and other 'totty' as it was called, did quite well too.

I also started a little cleaning job for a house dweller round the corner.

'Listen to me! House dweller! I was getting used to this strange language. Apart from a few words such as chovihanni, which took me ages to understand.

And yes Jake used to call me it, and no I didn't realise it meant 'old witch!' of course Jake laughed when he said it, and ran away, cheeky bastard!

By now my pride and joy had come along, and I stayed at home and looked after him instead of totting.

I named him Daniel. In fact I called him that from the second I conceived!

Thank goodness he wasn't a girl!

Standing at my window I could see the area in and around our site. There were a few houses dotted about

at the top of the road, but the rest were caravans. Some were chalets which are double the size of normal vans, but I loved our little pemberton caravan. It was only 34 foot long but it was home.

One day we decided to walk to the nearest town to sell some scrap. This journey would take us through some pretty little villages, and as it was warm and sunny, I grudgingly agreed to go with him.

Jake had been busy making a huge flat barrow. It had two wheels underneath the middle and a couple of handles.

'Get on then!'

Boy it was hot! I could feel the sweat dripping down my back. I couldn't remember the last time it was this boiling.

I wasn't in the mood for a long walk, but curiosity got the better of me

'What?' walking down the steps I suddenly spotted the weird contraption courtesy of Jake and his hammer!

'Get on! And I'll walk you and the chav to the scrap yard!'

Jake grinned. 'don'tcha think I can do it?'

Now Jake wasn't very big but he was wiry. He had muscles on his arms but was he up to pushing us?

Running my hand over the wood I could feel that it was pretty smooth. No splinters then.

'What about Dan? How can he sit on it?'

'Easy!' Jake rushed indoors, then back out holding a cushion. 'Sit him on that!' he said, triumphantly.

'This had better be good or else...!' I shook my head and went back indoors to grab my son.

'Well here goes nothing!' I plonked myself down on the cushion and placed my son in the middle of my lap. Nappy bag, check. Buggy, check........!

Fingers crossed, double check!

And we were off!

Thank goodness the road was flat, no potholes. We were walking through countryside.

I closed my eyes and held onto Dan. He was nearly asleep so I began to relax.

The suns warmth made me drowsy. The trundling of the barrow set up a rhythm of bump smooth bump smooth.....

'Ow!'

I jumped!

'What?' squinting in his direction I could see him rubbing his knee.

'whatcha do?'

'Banged me bloody leg on the 'andle! That bloody 'urt!'

Peace was shattered. But I did laugh!

'That's it, go on, laugh even though me leg nearly fell off!'

So what did I do? Laughed even more!

Jake started hopping on one leg, a pained expression on his face that made my son chuckle, his little face screwed up showing up his one tooth!

We must have looked a sight! A man jumping around on one leg, a baby cackling and screeching with laughter and me with tears in my eyes laughing so much!

Eventually we all calmed down, and peace reigned once more.

'Can you go on? Or do you want me to walk?' *'hope not!* I thought.

'Na you're alright.' swinging his arms to get the circulation going, he leaned over and grabbed the handles. Lifting us, he started to walk.

Sometimes Jakes ideas are not quite the er, well lets just say, best! He thinks he can do it, but as anyone would tell you, its not that easy pushing a barrow with an adult, a baby and a ton of iron on it!

To be fair, this time was different.

The sun was warm on my arms. It was a twilight world of light and shadow. The trees dappled with sunlight leaving trails behind my eyes.

I could hear bees buzzing away collecting nectar. And in the distance a stream tinkled over rocks. The smell was pure summer flowers and cooking from nearby houses.

It was Heaven. If Heaven is a gypsy pushing a wagon with a heavyweight on its back!

But too soon we arrived at the scrapyard.

'Help me with this will ya?' Jake dragged the bag of scrap off the barrow and headed towards the main gate of the scrap dealers.

After giving him a hand I was at a loss what to do. By this time my son was getting a bit weepy, he needed changing and a feed.

Luckily I had taken his bottle and nappy bag with me. Looking around to find a suitable place to do what was needed, I noticed a woman heading my way. Smiling, she opened the trunk of her car and beckoned me over.

I didn't know her, but she had the gypsy looks. Dark skin and long black curly hair, earrings jangling down her neck.

Wandering over, I gave her a smile.

'Well dawdy' she said, 'What's you doing here with a chavi in a barrow then?'

'Chavi?'

It takes a while to understand the gypsy accent. The only way I can describe it is like skimming a stone across water. The words seem to jump and not quite touch the ground.

'We're just bringing in some scrap to...'

'Well, you come a me and I see what I got in me boot o' me car,'

Before I had a chance to say no, she took hold of the pushchair and started cooing at Dan. 'Ah bootiful babby, booty blue eyes ya got there!'

Dan reached out and grabbed her finger, his eyes got bigger and bigger then a great big grin split his face.

'She must be nice then, I thought. 'my sons a great judge of character!'

We reached the car and when she opened the boot I couldn't believe my eyes!

Reaching in, she pulled out about three bags of brand new baby clothes, and handed them to me.

'That's for da sprog, and I won't take no for an answer, we's has to look after our own.'

She grinned and got back in the car. Turning the engine, she revved up and drove away.

I was astounded and humbled.

When Jake came back and saw me standing there, mouth open, he wondered what the hell was wrong.

'That woman,' I said pointing at the car, 'just handed me about 200 pounds worth of baby clothes!'

I turned to him and eyebrows raised, went on.

'Do you know her?'

Jake just laughed and picked up a small white jacket that would fit my son perfectly.

Shrugging his shoulders he turned to me and said,

'I don't need to know her personally, its just what we do!'

Well who knew?

I continued to be amazed at the generosity of the gypsies.

I soon found a toilet and quickly changing my sons soiled nappy.

Grabbing him under one arm, the buggy under the other I headed back out to Jake and the barrow.

What a good days work!

Chapter 4

Every year the fairground came to town. We would get dressed up in our best 'Sunday' clothes and me Jake and Dan, would head out to see what was what.

We soon reached the fairground. I noticed that it was full of gypsies.

The second we walked onto the field Jake was off!

Soon he was back. With him was an older man. His hair was slicked back, black and shiny, and the multi coloured scarf he wore round his neck made his face look darker.

'Let's have a look at the chav then.' His voice was gravelled and the gypsy burr was there.

And lets face it, he was fit! And we're not talking gymnastics fit either!

That's the one thing about gypsy men, boy are they gorgeous? Well yes they are!

The amount I have met over the years that can turn your innards to jelly just by looking at you is far to many to count!

Get my point?

I smiled and thought of the old English myth Weyland Smith.

There are loads of tales and fairy stories about the mysterious gypsy blacksmith who lures young women into the forest using his fairy magic.

The girls would hear the pounding of hammer on metal, and seek out the sound.

There, in the forest was a sight to be seen!

An old horse drawn vardo, a huge crackling fire, and a man.

Tall, muscles shining with sweat as he nailed a shoe onto a horse. A look of deep concentration on his face.

Magic was thick in the air as the man turned round and smiled.

'Come into the warmth my lady, sit by my side.'

The young girl was in his spell. As she got closer she began to pant and her dress would suddenly feel too tight.

Her fingers found the buttons and one by one they would pop open. And soon the dress would fall.......

'Nell!'

I jumped!

'What?'

'Are you going deaf woman? I said, does Dan want to go on a ride?' Jake glared at me.

'Jeesh! Going bright red in the face, I mumbled 'yes of course.' and stepped back out of the way!

The man grinned at me, a gold tooth shining in his mouth. I dared a look at his eyes.

He knew! Bloody hell! He could read my mind, oh crap cakes!

'I'll er....... go and have a go on the waltzer, okay?' turning I shot behind a stall selling burgers. My face still felt like it was on fire. 'I need a drink, big time!' and slipped around the other side of the stall and asked for a Coke.

And that was the trouble. Let me tell ya! Gypsy men have this...something. Don't ask me what it is, but its dangerous. In a good way and lets face it, in a bad way too!

I think it must be the touch of danger mixed with the unknown. Even when I married Jake and began the routine of married life I could still feel this something.

Its in the air when you meet gypsies. In reality of course its probably just imagination and boredom that makes us feel that way. But maybe not!

Anyway, back to the fair. Eventually I emerged fully confident that my...error? Glitch? Whatever, had gone and so I smiled my smile and came face to face with Jake and the man again.

Phew! This time I was in control. I gave him an aloof smile and turned to Jake.

'Where to now?'

Jake handed Dan to me and said goodbye to the man whose name I now found out was Steven.

We didn't pay a penny in rides for my son.

This gypsy community was awesome!

It was like being in an exclusive club.

No rules, just be friendly and fair.

I walked around the grounds waiting for Dan to get off the ride, and as I sat down I noticed something that made me laugh!

Every single fair worker seemed to know everybody. But straining my ears I could hear them.

And boy was it funny!

'Ay I know Ben, he's related to Joe's mother's fathers sister ain't he?'

And...

'I remember you, didn't you go to that school round the corner from Jim's 'ouse? You must be cousin john's boy then!'

Of course it was all said and done with a twinkle in the eye and a slap on the back.

Laughing to myself I let myself relax.

My son went on all the rides, got free candy floss and had a whale of a time!

I remember that day very well. It was one of the best.

I got to meet great aunts once removed.

Uncles who were only uncles by a marriage because their aunts were related.

And so many kids that I couldn't remember one of their names.

But it was family. Sort of!

As the day wore on I was tired but happy. We had enjoyed it. My son was asleep in the buggy, and Jake said it was time to go.

We went home with the same amount of money in our pockets as when we left. Kushti day!

Chapter 5

At this point I think its time to mention my upbringing. Throw a bit of light on the subject so to speak!

I was brought up to behave, never show my parents up and darn well be polite to neighbours! In plain English, be a lady!

When I was at school I was pretty much bullied from the first day I stuck my head around the classroom door!

The first person to start on me was an ugly little boy who constantly picked his nose.

I was five years old, yet I knew this was wrong, and yuck!

So I told on him.

And that was that. He kicked me, I ran yelling to the teacher and after that was ten years of hell by different kids, different schools and different teachers who didn't give a damn.

Till one day when I was pushed too far. A girl named Jane, stopped dead in front of me in the corridor to the library and stepped backwards kicking out at my leg.

I flipped!

I grabbed the bitch by the hair, threw her up against the headmasters wall and kept thumping her till she screamed for mercy!

That did it. No more bullying. Well, apart from a stupid cow who didn't get the memo. She tried kicking me too but I grabbed her leg and tipped her in the pond just for being deaf and stupid!

Others had got the message. She was to dumb to take notice!

Maybe that's why I left school at sixteen, got a job straight away in an office then went straight off the rails!

I stayed out till 3 am every weekend, flirted, kissed danced and played around with so many guys I couldn't even remember their names the next morning!

So when I got to 19 and met gypsy Jake, my mother presumed it was another 'phase' I was going through!

As I mentioned before, well, my mother was horrified!

My dad on the other hand thought it was the funniest thing he had ever seen!

And my dad had a chuckle on him that was so funny nobody could sit around being angry for long! Boy did he laugh!

'Trust Nell' he said, then laughed again!

I did miss them so when I moved out, but my life was so different living with Jake that I never had time to think on it too much.

And then there was my boy. Still a sprog in my tummy but I was growing bigger and bigger every day.

Did I say that I was pregnant before I got married? No? Ah, well that's another blip in my 'tell ma everything' story!

Well would you? No, thought not! That came later.

Chapter 6

Our caravan wasn't very big. It was only a 30 footer, a Pemberton vardo with a rounded end, and no main drainage.

But that was cool because there was a toilet block directly opposite our van.

Talking of toilets.....!

'What the hell is that?'

Jake was on the step holding a rather strange contraption in his hand.

Trying to look over his shoulder, I nearly fell out the door!

'Hold up will ya? Just give me a minute!'

'There!' Jake handed me the object.

Grinning, he said, 'well? What da ya think? Any good?'

There, in my hand was the fanciest bucket I had ever seen! The bottom half was painted green and around the top was …..fur? Was that fur?

I stared at him, dumbstruck!

'What the.?'

'Its a toilet!' he said, triumphantly.

'Its a....what?'

In the old days people would have put a chamber pot under the bed for night time peeing.

But no, not Jake. His invention was glorious, startling and downright, well posh!

I had my very own luxury portaloo!

Grinning he went on, 'at least you won't get cold at night when doing your business!'

Not a lot stumps me, but that did!

'But I only have to walk across the road and.....'

He interrupted me.

'What at 3 in the mornin? You don't know who's out there, you could get raped or something!' folding his arms he stuck up his nose and nodded.

'Who the hell is going to rape me at 3 am on the caravan site while I'm pissing, for goodness sake?'

But he had that look. So I was stuck with super loo!

And yes he was right. And no I didn't want to go traipsing out in the middle of the night.

And yes, it was warm and comfortable. A bugger not to get pee on the seat though!

Jake was good like that. Always trying to make me comfortable, especially with the little one on the way.

I remember when he brought me a cot and high chair for the babe and I wasn't even showing yet!

'Its a good un'!'

Handing it to me, he grabbed one of the legs and turned it on its side.

'Old Bill had it for his grand kids, its more than thirty years old. Good innit!'

It was made of wood. Shiny with age. Dark spots dotted the tray with years of spilled food. But it was good and sturdy.

Raising my eyebrows I looked at Jake.

'Clever little bugger aint ya?'

He laughed at my 'common voice' I used to speak like that when I wanted him to know he had done something nice.

It always made him smile.

And yes, when my son was old enough he settled into that high chair as though it was built for him.

My Jake. Good, bad, dumb and sometimes clever. But everything done with a smile.

Oh he could get grumpy, mind. Sometimes his face had a scowl on it that would turn milk sour. Kids would run away from his miserable face. Or so I told him!

But most times he was happy, and downright hilarious with it.

Mind you he was a lazy sod. It never dawned on me that he wouldn't try to get a 'proper' job.

'I do my copper and my other totty an' that will bring in the money, so don't you be getting stressed now not with the chavo on the way!'

Talking about the chav.........

The day I went into labour was probably one of the funniest, painful and rewarding days ever.

I cry with laughter even now when I think about it!

Jake was snoring his head off in the caravan bedroom. It was 6 in the morning, and I had been having pains all night. But not so bad that I couldn't get to sleep.

But then around five I had a huge contraction and scooted out of bed gasping, 'Jake wake up, Jake!'

But he just carried on sleeping.

As the pains didn't seem to be getting stronger, I decided to get up and see what was what.

I even started washing up the dishes in the sink.

I thought that if I was standing up I had more chance of knowing whether this 'was it' or just false pains.

Most pregnant women know the agony of rushing to hospital only to discover that they were having 'pangs' and not the real thing.

So I decided to wait and see.

I was just drying up the last plate when Jake emerged from the bedroom scratching his head.

'Whatcha doin?' he said with the stunned look of a man just dragged from sleep.

'I'm washing up, what's it look like?'

'Why?'

I looked at him.

'You better get the case ready, and run down to the phone box and call the ambulance while I finish up here.'

With that, I gently put the cups and plates away, then put down the tea towel.

'Well? What you waiting for?' crossing my arms I stared at him.

I'll give Jake his credit. The look on his face went from puzzlement, to alarm, fright, then sheer panic.

'Oh shit!' he said, then lunged for the bedroom door.

Grabbing his trousers he hopped around the room trying desperately get his legs in the holes. At the same time holding his T shirt in the other hand.

'Get out of the way, out! Water, give me water!'

With that he shoved past me, grabbed a glass filled it from the plastic water bucket, downed it in one,

poured some water into his hand, scrubbed his face and shot out the door.

Without his shoes. All I could hear was......

'Ouch, bugger it! Bollocks, fuck off.....' as he ran down the road.

Me? I just calmly sat down on the chair and waited for the ambulance!

It came before Jake got back.

But just as I was about to be carted off I heard 'Hey wait for me'!

And there was Jake, a huge grin on his face, racing up the road.

'Where have you been? I feel like my stomach's about to pop out my mouth, and you are out there bloody talking to the neighbours like king bloody Tut showing off his latest sprog! I ain't even had it yet!'

Now, I don't usually swear but when you feel like you are about to give birth to E.T you tend to start losing your decorum!

Jake, looking suitably chastised, climbed into in and took a seat beside me.

But soon we all calmed down and headed of to the local maternity hospital.

My son was born after fifteen hours of hard labour, and boy was it hard!

Crap cakes! I had never felt so much pain! Why didn't any one warn me? I would have kept my legs shut!

Of course Jake didn't get away with it. No pain? Oh yes! I made sure he had pain! Well, not deliberately you understand!

Two broken fingers should do it, poor Jake!

He insisted I hold his hand! What's a girl to do?

Serves him right for getting me in this state!

But there was another victim.

A nurse!

I didn't mean to do it, but......

'Put your feet on my side, and push! No, push harder!'

so I did.

Big time.

Last I saw of her was when she flew across the room and hit the wall!

She got up, brushed herself down and gave a very tentative smile. 'Okay, its fine!' in her lovely Chinese accent.

I remember yelling, 'sorry! oh fuck it, OUCH!'

Then, amongst all the noise blood and pain, out slid this little scrap of humanity pulling a face and my old man yelling 'He's got the Elvis lip'!

And to my astonishment, he had!

You know, that face he pulls when he sings and says 'Uh ha yeah!'

Elvis not the baby. Keep up!

As Jake used to sing in the pubs as an Elvis impersonator...yes I know, stop laughing......!

He was pleased as punch!

After that all I wanted was a cup of tea and to hold my lovely new baby.

After taking him off to be cleaned up, and checked, the nurse came back and handed him to me.

I could smell the baby powder on his little body. Breathing in his scent for the first time.

He had big blue eyes, and his head was covered in silver white down. Beautiful.

Everybody else could sod off. Including Jake. He had totally forgotten his broken fingers by this point.

But trust me, over the years he has never forgotten it. Usually spouting for all and sundry;

'Yeah she was bloody strong mush, I tell ya she was going to make a great Daj!'

A Daj?

Turns out its the gypsy word for mother.

I was a mother!

Its a strange feeling. But one of the most rewarding in the world.

A week later, we were home.

Chapter 7

Little did I know how much room a tiny baby would take up!

'Jake, pass me the tub will ya?' clutching my son to my breast I tried grabbing the bowl but it was too far out of my reach.

He brought it over and watched me as I placed my son, very gingerly into the water.

I was still getting used to this mother lark, and I was scared to death that I would drop my precious boy.

'You don't have ta clutch him like that, he won't break! Give 'im 'ere!' he reached across and took Dan from me.

'See just hold his head like this,' turning round so I could see what he was doing, 'and rub him wiv' the cloth like this.'

To my total astonishment, my son, who five minutes before was wailing at the top of his voice, stopped, burped, and grinned his toothy grin at Jake!

Seeing my surprise he said 'You forget, I got five brothers and sisters, all of them younger than me. I used to help me ma out with them!'

Funny how I never even thought of that. I knew that he was the eldest. Well, the second born, but didn't realise that he was so involved

I relaxed a bit. It was good to know that I wasn't the only one my son could rely on now.

My family lived a few miles away, so it wasn't a case of popping next door for help, unfortunately.

So washing changing and general panic button situations were handled pretty well, considering!

On the other hand washing out baby nappies or diapers in a single wash tub was, well, let's just say pretty smelly!

Jake of course left all that to me. Being a typical gipsy he thought it was all 'Woman's work!!' cheers Jake!

Luckily I had been given an old wash boiler. Not exactly a washing machine but it was better than nothing.

When my son soiled his nappy, I would have to shove it in a bag, cross the road and go into the toilet block where I could scrap the poo off into the toilet.

Then back I would go. Getting a bucket, the nappies would be shoved in with disinfectant and bleach.

Finally, they would be put into the boiler just to make sure there wasn't any germs left.

Yes maybe it was 'over the top' but he was my pride and joy. Nothing was going to make him ill.

Fingers crossed!

Chapter 8

One day when I was hanging out washing, I could hear a right old ding dong going on across the road.

Sorry for those who don't understand gypsy crossed with cockney.....

Ding dong definitions; Arguments, punching, swearing and general mayhem!

Yeah got it? Anyway.......!

I put the washing down and headed for my 'nosy' spot, by the front gate. They couldn't see me, but I could see them! Hah!

Now you only hear a gypsy call another one a hedgemumper when that person has annoyed them, big time!

But I could hear the word being bandied about across the road.

'Ooh! Wonder who's pissed them off?' I stuck my nose through the fence trying to get a better look.

I had asked Jake a few days before, what a hedgemumper was.

'Why do you want to know that for?' he looked puzzled then laughed.

'Just trying to learn your gypsy ways!' I sniffed and carried on reading.

'I'll have to write it all down for ya. Either that or go and piss someone off, then you'll find out!' this was followed by a roar of laughter!

Anyway, back to the present.

My nose felt like it was getting longer and longer as I tried desperately to listen.

I know what you're thinking. I really do. What's with the nose? Well, ya see, if I put my ear to it, it was too high. If I tried looking through it the angle was wrong.

So I had to follow my nose. So to speak. Yeah I know, we gorgi's are a funny bunch!

Now, gypsies are nice people. But just like the rest of us they can get double peeved if someone treads on their toes.

Which someone obviously had this time.

To be honest what with all the yelling going on I really couldn't see or hear much.

Eventually the gate opposite opened and a scruffy looking man walked out, yelling over his shoulder,

'Ya stinking bastard! Don't come round mine again!' and stomped off in a huff.

I went back indoor telling myself to mind my own business.

But it did get me thinking.

Gypsies are like the rest of us. We mind our own business until someone invades our territory.

The trouble is, because gorgio's and gypsy's have different lifestyles it can cause rifts among a community.

I don't know who that guy was, but because I heard that word, hedgemumper, I would imagine that he was a non gypsy, or maybe a pikie.

There is one thing that stands out in the gypsy community and that is their togetherness.

Not only do they help each other but if a gorgi, like me, decides to marry a gypsy then I automatically become one of them.

Not only do they give us carpets and cups, they also love to give advice!

Some of it is given with a twinkle in the eye! And some can be quite sobering.

'Just remember Nell luvvie, not everyone 'ere loves gorgio's.' that was the advice from old Vic. Smoking his pipe and gazing into the distance.

I always listened to him. He was a lovely man.

And yes, not all gypsy's liked us!

Take for example Jakes aunt Lina. She took an instant dislike to me.

According to her way of thinking, 'Gypsies should only marry their own kind, who do ya t'ink you are tekkin' one of our men's away?'

This was said at a birthday party down the town hall. I can't remember who's. A cousin of a cousin once removed probably!

Anyway.........

So I smiled and said 'Well I do love him, isn't that enough?'

She stared at me. Oh boy did she stare! If I had been a lesser being I would have shrivelled under that gaze!

But no I am my mother's daughter. So with a swift shudder, and a sweaty palm, I stared her right in the eye.

'I am not tekkin...er taking one of your men. We are going to live on the site, and I will make him very....'

Before I had a chance to finish the sentence she grabbed my wrist, her beady little eyes squinting at my hand!

I tried to pull away but boy, was she strong for an old witch, er woman!

'I can see your future and it ain't what you's want it to be,' She snarled.

Pulling my hand even closer to her face she went on,

'I can see's at least three children, one chavo and two chavi, then him will leave ya!'

With this she shrieked with laughter.

'Yep old witch!' sniffing, I pulled my hand away and turned my back to her.

So, I was going to have three kids, one boy and two girls eh? Then Jake is going to leave me.

Sorry love Crystal ball alert! Wrong!

I had one boy, admitted I had three miscarriages but Jake never left me. However many times I wanted him to!

His family were like that. Very suspicious. Oh don't get me wrong! Most of them were welcoming, but there was always that.... something.

To be fair, when you have been persecuted by a race of people for centuries it doesn't do to trust them straight away. I got it. But it was weird being picked on for being white, British and gorgio!

Now I know what it felt like. And its not nice.

Talking of family, I haven't really mentioned his brothers and sisters.

To be honest I didn't really have a lot to do with them. But I did get on with his older sister.

Jakes mother was a gorgio like me. She passed away too young. Fifty three years old.

His dad on the other hand, was a scary man! He was a stereotypical gypsy.

Dark hair, swarthy looks and a huge laugh.

I never really knew how to take him. But we never really saw them much.

Maybe a trip into Maidenhead to visit once a fortnight. Then we lost touch.

Shame really.

I would love my son to have been more involved with them. But it wasn't to be.

Some barriers you just couldn't cross!

Chapter 9

We had some laughs in that old caravan.

And the neighbours were really nice too. Well most of them!

There was one incident when I threatened to strangle a newbie gorgi!

Yeah you heard me! By this time I saw myself as 'One of them!'

Gypsies.

And it was at this point I realised that some gorgi's were far more ignorant than any Romany.

Me and Jake had decided to go up in the world a bit. There was a lovely brand new Vardo on site, it was two up from where we were living.

Levi, another Gypsy yelled through our window one day.

'Quick you better get in there afore another person grabs it!'

But first we had to sell our old Vardo.

Mind you, it was in good condition. Jake had painted the whole caravan a lovely blue.

The piping round the top of the caravan was black, painted with a tiny thin artist brush.

Jake was very artistic. Where I would throw the brush away after two seconds of frustration, Jake could sit their for ages putting a tiny piece of wood on a model caravan.

So the Vardo was kushti, and we had a few people interested.

Eventually we managed to find two gorgi's who were willing to move in at the right price.

They said that they would sort out their funds and get back to us.

But did they? No!

They did the dirty on us!

While we were still waiting for them to sort out their money, they sneaked behind our back and bought the new caravan that we were going to move into!

I was as mad as a ferret on a bike!

What made it worse was the smug look on the cows face!

Then she had the nerve to stand in the vardo window and laugh!

Well I lost my rag, and leaped over the garden fence and ran up the stairs to her door!

"Come out you thieving cow! That's a dirty trick! Thump! "If I get my hands on you.....!" Thump!

(not her head, just the door!)

Next second Jake and Tim were dragging me backwards and telling me not to show them up!

"Chavaia! God you's got a chib on ya! Stop showing us up you divi rackli! You sound like you got the beng in ya!"

Oh gawd! Now I done it!

When the men start yelling Romany insults you know you're in trouble!

By the way? What they said was roughly translated as, 'Stop, you got a big mouth, you stupid girl you sound like you got the devil in ya.' Oops!

Suitable chastened I headed in doors and opened a bottle of wine.

Now, I used to be a good girl. Quiet as can be. I never argued, fought or kicked off in any way.

But that pissed me off. Big time. And yes I was suitably embarrassed and annoyed at myself.

Hence the wine. Red, chilled and yum!

I crept over to the window.

I could hear various words in English but the rest was a mixture of Romany, English and swearing.

Methinks its time for me to keep my head down for a while.

To be honest I am not sure exactly what came over me! I don't act like that!

In fact I was so badly bullied at school that for me to turn and attack like that was, well, very unusual to say the least!

But to be fair, I was deeply disappointed at what they had done to me.

The vardo was tiny, my son was growing up and needed more space and I thought....well I thought the van was mine. So I lost it.

Maybe all the stress of leaving home and changing cultures had hit me more than I realised.

It was time to calm down, think of my family and just get the hell on with it!

They can keep the caravan, we would be fine where we were.

After that things got back to normal, with Jake going overboard to help out with our son. Mind you it was funny when I asked him to change a nappy!

"What? You have got to be kidding me! I ain't changing no chavo with a stinky backside! I will do other stuff but not that!"

So I got him sorting out the rubbish. Then we moved the furniture what there was of it, to get more room.

After a couple of hours the whole caravan was spick and span! It looked gorgeous in fact!

"Well done Jake, that looks real frumos! (lovely). Time to put our feet up!

Chapter 10

It was mid summer. Such a poignant time of the year. It always seemed like a dream.

It was that lovely carefree time. The sound of bees could be heard buzzing around the flowers, children were playing and lawns were being mown.

Sunlight on water. Sparkling, tinkling. Fish running high and mosquito's flying. It was all sound, sight, and smell.

The flowers were gorgeous that year. Jake had planted some roses the year before, and now they were in full bloom.

But underneath the touch of summer was always the sadness that autumn was just around the corner.

Sitting in the garden I could hear birds clacking and tweeting, and the smell of the grass invading my nostrils left a tickle. I love the scent of green. Grass, trees, hedges, and pine.

Soon the nights would be drawing in. Then October would be here, and with it one of Jakes 'not very good' ideas!

I smiled. Jake wasn't very good at playing tricks. Something always seemed to go wrong!

As the days drew in we would start to make plans for Halloween.

'What we goin' to do about costumes this year?'

Jake was cleaning an old copper boiler just outside the caravan door.

Um not sure to be honest, do we have to dress up?'

I was once again changing my son so I didn't see the laugh on Jakes face.

'I got a great idea!'

Now, when Jake gets an idea I start to panic!

But to be fair, sometimes they were really good ones.

So this time I will let him get on with it.

I can't be that bad. Can it?

Oh dear! I wish I hadn't!

He didn't say anything else, but he had that look on his face!

'I'll tell you nearer the time!' and off he went with his broken bits and pieces.

The summer turned to autumn.

Golden leaves settled gently onto the grass. The smell was warm woodsmoke and chilled air.

We were sitting outside our Caravan making the most of it before it turned really cold.

I think this time of year was the most beautiful.

The multi coloured leaves on the trees looked magical.

Each day they would change to a different hue, and then gently fall to the floor.

I would collect them and then me and Dan would sit at the kitchen table gluing them onto a piece of paper ready to stick on the wall.

Dan's little hands covered in paste, laughing as I stuck a leaf to my forehead.

Soon tiredness overcame him and I slipped him into his cot for an afternoon nap.

Jake was doing what he does best. Not a lot!

He fiddles with something to make it work better, but just breaks it instead.

I went outside to collect the washing.

'I got an' idea!'

Wait for it!

'Yes?
I know what's coming.
It's one day away from Halloween, and the gypsies liked to play tricks on each other.
 Just like us gorgi's.
But there was one difference.
It usually involved money, or belongings. They would set up a test, and whichever one of them won, they would earn a bit of vonga.

 But it's got to be a good idea. The plan was, you had to play a joke on someone. And it had to be good.
There were no rules.
Word always got around after the event then they would all get together and decide the winner.
Past winners were pretty innovative.
 For example, some of the ideas were simple.
Phone and say that they had won some money.

Or, phone them and yell someone had stolen their car and they had better come quick!
Various jokes were tried and tested. Others fell by the wayside.
 'Oh yeah, what's that then?'

   I peer at him over the top of the old mangle which was making a clunking noise. It was on its way out. I couldn't afford a washing machine so a mangle was very handy.
I waited for the great idea.
Hope it wasn't like last years disaster! I remember it well.
Jake decided to sneak into one of the gypsies gardens and steal a hub cap off their car.
Trouble was, he forgot about the dogs...ouch!
Anyway back to the present!

I could see light beginning to glow behind his eyes and the gears grinding into place.
Jake wasn't the quickest tool in the box if you get my meaning but when he got an idea he went for it. Hammer and tongs so to speak.
He started to grin. Uh oh wait for it.....!

'You know that old Indian costume my uncle Alby gave me after his cousins wedding? I'm going to put that on and give Tim a scare! I'll frighten the life outta him when I knock on his door!'
Well that can't go wrong, can it?
   Let's take time out for a little bit of history here. Jakes ancestors came from India. I know most people believe the word gypsy comes from Egypt, but in fact the original Romany's came from India.
 Anyway I digress.
'Okay that sounds quite a good idea in theory, so what's the plan?'
"Well Tim mentioned the other day that he had got behind in his land rent and he was scared that they would send someone round.'
'So......!'
 Grinning, he went on.

'Well I may just knock on his door and.....' he laughed.
 I thought for a moment.
Okay, but will Tim see the joke?
'Lets finish off here and go in and find that costume!'
I put the mangle away and stood up.
   Tims' caravan was adjacent to ours and I could see his wife pegging out the clothes on the wash line. She was smiling and nodding her head.
So Tim had to be there then, but I couldn't see him from where I was standing.

Looking up, she spotted me and yelled out 'Hiya, are you two's comin' over 'ere later for a spot o' dinner?'
 Damn! I had forgotten that we had been invited over. Hope Jake keeps his mouth shut, or doesn't decide to do it tonight!
   Diving indoors to get changed, I yelled at Jake to get a move on.
Living on a site wasn't as easy as being a house dweller. It took longer to get organised, bathed and so on.
  The caravan site was circular. We were on the right hand side coming in from the main road, and there was middle circle where Tim and Belle lived.

The toilet and shower block were approximately 20 feet up the road so it was easy to get to. Only thing that got on my wick was having to traipse up to the top of the site to get to the water tap.

   We were a happy community though.
 Most of us were gypsies but there were quite a few gorgies on site too.
We all got on pretty well apart from a few skirmishes between gypsy families who had different ideas for the same things!
 Yeah I know, confusing!
   Tim and Belle were our main friends, but there were a few other friendly neighbours too.
We got together a few nights a week to play cards, chat or just have a laugh.
   At 7-o-clock we shut the front door and walked across the road and knocked on their window. I carried Dan under my arm, and Jake took the carrycot.
  'Hiya, just us!'
'Ah come in, come in! That's it, take a pew. Si tut bocklo'?'
'Na we are fine thanks, we ate before we came over, but a nice cuppa tea would be good, ta.'
'By the way Belle congrats on your sisters new baby, what did she have?'

'Aye it was a lil' chavi God bless her soul and she is a beauty!'
'Have they named her yet?'
Belle put the cup down and sighed.
'Ah, it aint like it wos back then ya no's. These days the man can sit in the 'ospital and see the babe the second its born not like afore.'
 She leaned forward and picked up a photo that was lying on the table in front of her.

'This is me and me mam, our sister Tolly and my brother Plato, he was a bugger he was.' She smiled.
'When we wus born it was different. Me ma had a new tent put up just for the baby to be born.
No mush was allowed near it, and for a few weeks after the birth the woman won't allowed ter cook any food cos she was mochadi (dirty) till the babe was christened ya see. It was called churching. For the mother I mean.' She sighed.
  'When the babe was christened the father could hold the bairn and the tent would be burned to the ground.'
'Ah, them days were the best.'

She had a far away look in her eye and at that moment she wasn't a young woman. In her eyes I could see all the women who had come before her, feel her pain at the changes modern life had brought to them all.

The yearning in her face was so sad to see. This was the early 1980's, only a few years before they would be taking to the road either driving a brand new caravan or an old traditional vardo.

  In that moment it was as though I could feel the rush of the wind, hear the clip clop of the horses hoofs and the 'Wey hey boy, come back come back good grai,' from the man who was up front holding the reins.

  I don't think I realised until that point how much these lovely people had given up. The warm summers out on their vans jostling up the horses, the children running out in front so excited to get to the fields and start picking fruit and flowers to be sold to the markets, either by their fathers or the farmer who owned the fields.

  Every year they went back on the same route, meeting up with their family members and friends, sitting round the camp fire of an evening laughing, dancing and playing their guitars and drums.
And in the winter months huddling together in the vans with their stews and soups keeping them warm.
  It was a hard life, but one they all loved so much.
I could feel my eyes getting misty and blinked it away.
The room seemed to shift as thought it had been holding its breath back in time. And only became alive when Belle placed the photo back on the table.
  'Her names Mercy,' Belle said, and stood up.
I jumped, and looked up. For a second I had forgotten I was with company.
  'Mercy?' I said.
' Yes, we called her Mercy in the hope that the good Lord will have Mercy on her in the years to come, what wiv all the comin' and goin, you understand?'
  She looked at me with a hard stare, and at that moment, I was no longer one of them, but a gorgi who belonged to the race of people who had tormented them for centuries.
'I understand Belle' I whispered.

Later that night I lay in bed thinking about what Belle had said. It must be so hard to change your lifestyle so drastically.
Look at me! I jumped feet first into a completely different way of life.
How was I coping? Well to be honest I wasn't sure. Some days it was easy. Other days I found myself standing around looking totally bemused at how different things were.

As I began to drift of to sleep I found myself smiling as I remembered the day when Jake and I crossed paths for the first time.

Chapter 11

June 1978 ....

I had been working in Maidenhead for three weeks. The job that I applied for turned out to be a nightmare, it sucked big time but I needed the money.

One day I decided to move my desk over to the window as the room was so dark even with the sun shining.
It was a heavy desk, but I was determined to move it, much to the amusement of my colleagues.
'Oh shut up! If you're going to laugh come and help me.' I grunted, and pulled it across the floor.
I got it in the right position, and with a huge sigh sat down and grabbed my coffee.
The window was wide open and I could hear the sound from the road.

I settled down to work only to hear someone singing outside. Curiosity got the better of me and I reached across to the window opened the catch, and flung it wide.

There below me, was a dark haired guy singing his way along the road, not taking any notice of the strange looks or smiles that came his way.
   I noticed that he was carrying a huge radio cassette on his shoulder.
I laughed. His voice was pretty good!
After lunch I kept thinking about him.
Who was he? Did he live round here?
A little voice in my head said 'Go and find out who he is!'
Oh yes what a great idea! Why not go up to a strange man and say 'Hiya loved your singing how's it going?'

So I put him to the back of my mind and carried on with my work.
  By the end of the day I was exhausted and not looking forward to the journey home on the train.
But my mind kept returning to that guy. Who was he?
Sitting in the train I looked out the window.
Did I really want to get involved with a complete stranger just because he looked interesting?
And once again that traitorous little voice said
 'Yes go on, you know you want to!'

  Why does my brain tell me one thing, when I try to do the opposite?
 But a part of me was excited!
Who is he? Where does he live? Is he even English? He did look foreign.
 I love the Mediterranean look. Dark hair warm skin and.....!
Oh for goodness sake Nell what are you thinking?
But that's the trouble with me. I don't think!
I go too fast and jump in before my brain has worked out the details. I need to sit down and weigh up the options.
   I had a habit of diving into relationships. Up until this point most of my conquests had just been casual. I had never had a long term boyfriend before.
What was I looking for? Seemed to me that something was yelling in my inner ear 'settle down!'
Oh yeah? At nineteen years old? Had I really go so apathetic and world weary at such a young age that I wanted to give up meeting guys and settle with a stranger?
Okay, most people would want a steady romance with all the trimmings.
I on the other hand was having too much fun!
So......what?

  I forgot about him when I got home. Or should I say, deliberately put him out of my mind.
Won't work. He's not part of my group. We live in different towns. And so on.
Round and round my brain it goes......
Of course, he may not want me! Never thought of that did I?
Oh hell! Go with the flow I say!

  On the way to work the next morning I was hoping that I would see him again from my office window.

Now its at this point, erm, that I have to point out that I am quite, cough.... short sighted!
In fact pretty much everything is a blur beyond 20 feet or so!
My point?

So the man I was staring at out the window on that first day wasn't quite so handsome as I thought.
Which turned out to be a good thing. In retrospect!
Now I know what you are thinking. Big headed cow!
But no, that's not the point I am trying to make.

If I had seen him up close, probably in my 19 year old way, I would have thought him ugly.
In other words I would have missed out on years of love kindness and laughter.
Looks ain't everything! And lets face I am not exactly an oil painting! As my mother would point out!

Anyway, as the story goes.....

I had been working at the Hell Hole as I called it, for around 6 weeks when a friend came up with an idea.......
'Stalk him? You want me to stalk him? What the hell sort of girl do you think I am? What if he gets annoyed and yells police?' I said, eyebrows raised.

'No you silly cow, find out who he is, then maybe stick a letter through his door!'
Pearl scratched her head and pulled a face.
'I mean, surely if he isn't interested he will still find it flattering to think a hot girl like you is chasing him?'
Hot girl my arse! I thought.
grabbing my brush I tried to untangle my hair. It does that after washing. Tangle I mean.

With that she took out her lipstick and applied deep red to her lips.
She looked really good.
I on the other hand would look like a vampire if I wore that colour. But then again I don't have dark mocha coffee skin and ringlets like she does.
I am blond, bottled of course, but blond, slim and pale.
A lot of guys think I am attractive, but after being bulled badly at school I was still waiting to see if I believe it or not.
Hence the nerves caused by Pearls great idea!

'Oh come on, it will be a laugh. What have you got to lose? Its Saturday, lets get on that train and go find!'
She laughed, looking so stunning I left my confidence firmly on the seat under my rather flat butt cheeks.

'Its alright for you' I said, 'You've got the nerve to do something like this but I.....'
'No buts, ifs or and's, we are going, now!'

And with that, she stormed out the door.
I chased after her.

We got on the train, and headed back to Maidenhead.
I was sweating like a stuck pig, and not because it was hot.
What if he laughs at me?
The train pulled into the station. I pressed the button to open the door.
I stepped down.
By this time my legs were getting slightly shaky. What the hell was I doing?

Chapter 12

I felt a shove between my shoulder blades and Pearl stepped forward with a huge grin on her face.
'Lets go girl!' And off she ran.
Great! I thought, and started to jog after her.

'We'll go this way, you said you think he lives up this road didn't you?'
'Pearl will you slow down! By the time I see him I am going to be so hot I'll pass out!'
I stopped, took a great gulp of air then looked around.

Now at this point I have to say it. I have never ever done anything like this before! I think I was hoping that we wouldn't find him, then give up and go for a drink. But it wasn't as easy as that.
Oh no, never is!
When Pearl got a bee in her bonnet, well she got a huge bee!

We chased around for two sweaty long hours! Where the hell was he? I thought he would be quite well known considering the er, rather large cassette he carried around on his shoulder!
After a few strange and sometimes blank looks I decided that enough was enough.
I would ask one more person if they knew him and if not then home I would go!
I was secretly hoping that Pearls mad dash and dating day would turn up a blank.
But what I didn't realise was one huge obstacle standing in our way!

The house we were standing in front of turned out to be none other than his house!
Gulp!
Oh boy!
There was a young woman digging her front garden. So, tentatively I coughed and asked if she knew the man I was looking for.
'Yes that young man lives next door! But I believe he is working at the fairground today.'
'Thank you.' I turned to Pearl.

'Ah well never mind, we'll leave it at that then.' and I started to walk back towards the railway station.

   Fairground?
I suppose I should have figured it out then and there. But no, I wasn't so quick back then as I am today. In hindsight I should have walked away and left the poor guy alone. Don't get me wrong, it wasn't because he was a gypsy, it was more the fact that I was jumping or trying to jump into a culture that I knew nothing about.

But I was curious. Like most people, I usually dated someone who was in my local pub or sports club. This was the first time I had deliberately searched for someone. So I was beginning to feel a bit, well, nervous!
 And I had an itchy feeling of wrongness going up and
 down my spine!
I could have walked away at that point, but no, Pearl decided that a letter would be appropriate. If not delivered in person, then shoved through the door!

  I grabbed a pen from my bag and found my notebook.
Scribbling down a few words of introduction and would you like to meet up etc, I folded it, stuck it in an envelope and thrust it through the letter box.
Oh hell and a high basket, in for a penny in for a pound as the old saying goes!

   To be honest I forgot about it over the rest of the weekend, and by Monday morning I went to work in my usual state of tiredness, crossed with resignation.

Half way through the morning the phone rang.
Now I should have felt some frisson of excitement as I leaned over to pick it up. But my brain was on dates, timetables and debits and credits.
'Hello? Is that Nell?'
'Yes speaking, can I help you?' I picked up a pen ready to take notes.
'Er yeah, its me, Jake? You er...left me a note asking to meet up? I wondered...um....if you'd like to go for a drink, or maybe coffee....or something.....?' at this point the voice dried up, and silence ensued.
Oh shit cakes! Oh bloody hell in a basket! It was him!
I began to sweat, big time.
What could I say? Saturday was saturated in sun, booze and fun.
Today was sober Monday!
I took a deep breath and.....
'Oh hi!' my voice squeaked two octaves higher than normal and I coughed to level it.
'Erm, yeah, that would be great!'
 No it won't, no no no.....

'Friday? Yes that's fine, where should we meet?'
'Tell me where you work and I'll meet you for lunch, is that okay?'
'Yep, that's great!' *Oh yes Nell go ahead and keep repeating yourself, why not? I'm sure he's really impressed!'*

That lovely little thing called subconscious in my brain had already started to tell me off and give me advice.
Always happens whenever I get nervous.
Trouble is, its not always the best advice!
At least I had four days to get ready. Panic, I meant panic. Same difference!
Then............
'No, tell ya what, I am coming down the town this dinner time, I'll come and get ya and we can go have a coffee, yeah? '
Silence.
'Oh hell in a basket! What do I say?'

'Um, yeah, that will be okay. One ish?' I dropped the pen, my hands sweaty and clammy.
'Yep, give me your work address and I'll see you then!'
I mumbled the name of the firm, and the road, said goodbye and put the phone down.
By this time the sweat had turned to ice cold fear.
I was sober. At work. And downright shy!
I watched the clock, its hands betraying me by going to fast until it was ten to the hour of hell.

Shutting down the PC I headed to the bathroom.
Splashing cold water on my face, I re-applied my make-up and pulled a comb through my hair.

Sniffing my armpits just in case, I sprayed liberal amounts of perfume from head to toe.
With a bit of luck he will be so knocked out with the smell he won't notice my blushing!
Phew! Breath, come on, breath!

I walked out of the office, down the stairs and headed towards the door.
I could see his outline through the misty glass windows and my last thought was, here goes!
Smile that's it, whatever happens, smile!
The door opened and I was out in the daylight. The sun bright on my face.
And here he was.
He was taller than I had initially thought. With black hair, Yum, bonus..! and and dark suit that looked like it was two sizes to big and had recently been stuck on a artists dummy.
Up close he was pretty ugly to be honest. But then I realised that it wasn't his face that was wrong, it was his hairstyle.
That'll have to go!
Yep, thanks brain, I'll sort it out, keep quiet!
He had gorgeous hair, hidden underneath a layer, two layers..? of brill cream, smarmed back in a greasefest of a fifties D.A. !
Look it up! Yep, that one!
We stared at each other.
Then he smiled and took my hand.
'Hiya,' he said.

I gulped. 'Hello.'
We started to walk down the road towards the town.
'Coffee?' he squeezed my hand. It was warm. My little fingers fitted perfectly.
   I rolled my hand into a ball, and he stretched his fingers and covered mine.
Warm, safe and protected. And I knew.
Just in that second I felt he was the one. It was the most natural feeling in the world.
Wow! So that's what it felt like!
He was ugly-ish, bad hair, skinny as hell but he was mine.
To be honest that first date didn't go that well. For starters I was so nervous I could have slid of the cafe seat with sweat! Sorry for being too basic, but yep it was true!
He, on the other hand seemed to take it in his stride.

   'Yeah, I found your note when I got back from the fair. Wondered what the hell it was!' he snorted with laughter, 'Yeah I thought it was a bill for somethin' I had forgot to pay! Was gonna throw it in the bin!'

 The grin spread across his face and totally transformed it.
Where before he was not particularly attractive, when he smiled his eyes twinkled and he had dimples In his cheeks and one in the middle of his chin.
I stared, fascinated.
Of course it wasn't that easy. He was rough as an uncut diamond. His language was interlaced with the most colourful words you could possibly hear!
Trouble was there was more swearing in one sentence than the actual sentence itself.
That would have to go before I introduced him to my mum! Yep, full language course followed by ettiquete lessons en Suisse!
   Was this the man I wanted to be with? Really? Whatever happened to nice, polite boy next door? Which was exactly what my mother wanted.
Literally!
   I found out that he shared a house with an old gay guy and his partner. Evidently Jake did not get on with his family.
Looking in his eyes I could see he was wary of me, but desperately wanting to reach out and trust.

   Soon it was time for me to return to work. So finishing up my coffee we headed back out the door.
I said goodbye to him, and with promise of phone calls, went inside.
Boy was I confused!
I realised at this point, that I would be taking on a huge risk with him. His culture, background and unspoken problems with his family.
Did I really want him?

   Over the next few days he rang me often. In fact he was pretty pushy to be honest and I began to panic.

   After one particularly embarrassing incident when he turned up at my house on a Sunday morning asking to see me, I thought no, I can't do this.

My parents didn't help. They thought he was rude to impose on a weekend like that. And to be honest I did think it was a bit much.

But for some reason, to this day I cannot fathom, I allowed him to push me forward more and more. Until one day when he asked me to marry him!

Before I had a chance to decide, my mouth said 'Yes'.

What the hell......?

Looking back, I realise that my subconscious knew what it wanted.

We were never apart from that day forward. Five months after meeting, we were married and off we went to live in a caravan on a gypsy site.

Chapter 13

And then I woke up and found myself back to the present.

My dream, reminiscing, call it what you will left a smile on my face.

That is until I realised that this bright new day was in fact the 31st October!

Halloween and Jakes great plan!

Here we go, this had better be good, or else.....!

At around 7 pm Jake decided that it was time for his grand plan to finally be on show. Oh dear!

'What are you going to do?'

I sat down and just stared at the transformation. It actually was pretty funny.

There right in front of me was an Indian Prince! All I could see was his teeth, stark white from the lamp against the dark background of the bedroom.
'What the hell?'

Gypsies originated in India and what with the turban, long blue robe and floppy slippers he looked like something from Aladdin. Yes I know Aladdin was Chinese but, you get my point!

'Okay go on then Einstein what's the plan?'

'No problem, I am just going to tap on Tims door and when he answers just say somethin' like, hello I have come to buy your caravan!'
Jake said grinning from ear to ear.

I wasn't so sure. I knew Tim, he wasn't the sort to take kindly to anyone knocking on his door at this time of night!
But we will see.

The saying 'stupid is as stupid does' tends to be Jakes byword.
I mean, its not as if he is really dumb, but sometimes his brain doesn't connect to his common sense. I could see this was going to go badly wrong, but I wasn't sure exactly how.

So like the good wife that I tried to be, I took myself outside the vardo, and sat on the top step so I could get a birds eye view.
   All I needed was a box of popcorn and a coke and it would be like Saturday night at the movie's.
Whether it was going to be a comedy or a murder was anybody's guess.

It was pretty dark at this point and as Jake walked across the road I realised that I wouldn't be able to see much.
I mean, knocking on a door wouldn't be a problem.
Would it?!

The moon suddenly appeared from behind the clouds and like a spotlight casting a full glow onto a stage full of actors, Jake suddenly appeared in front of the caravan door.
I could hear the knock, and suddenly a light appeared in the caravan hallway.

A face appeared and then I saw Tim waving his arms around his head. At this point the voices headed my way.

'Get away from me you stinking money grabbing bastard!'

With a yell, Jake shot backwards down the steps and headed for the gate.
 But he wasn't quick enough!
Next second I saw a fist come up and with one almighty punch Jake sailed through the air and hit the gate post!

'Yikes!' I began to run across the road.
'Tim, Tim stop! Its Jake!'
'Oh my God!'
By the time I got to the door, Jakes nose was pouring with blood and Tim was heading for another knockout!

'TIM ITS JAKE! STOP HITTING HIM!' I yelled and grabbed his arm.
For a second Tim just looked at me and was about to pull away when the light suddenly dawned on his face.
'Jake is that really you? You bloody stupid plank I coulda killed ya'! Tim shook me off and put his hand out to help Jake up.

Suddenly Tim started laughing!
'Ha ha you bloody stupid plonker! Whatcha think ya doin'?'
Jake was sitting on the grass a look of complete astonishment on his face, holding his nose which was pouring with blood.
Wiping it with his sleeve he turned to Tim.
'Ah but I got ya Tim, you didn't realise that it was a Halloween joke!' Said Jake trying to maintain some sort of dignity.
Tim's shoulders started to shake. And a snorting yell shot out of his mouth and he laughed.
'The jokes on you ya idjit! Its not Halloween yet, its tomorrow!' Tim turned away and stomped back into the caravan.

'Tomorrow?' Yelled Jake. Then turning to me said 'Why didn't you tell me you stupid rackli?'
Ooh, Jake was angry!
Oops!
'Erm, who's the stupid one?' I turned and walked away smirking to myself. 'I'm not the one with a bloody nose'!
And that was the end of the All Hallows comedy half hour!
And nobody calls me a stupid rackli! Boy was I going to make him suffer!

   Do you know, he nursed that swollen nose for two weeks! Grumbling and moaning, asking me in a pleading voice 'Can you get me a beer my sweet?' and 'I was um, wonderin' if ya would be so kind as to go and take the dog out as I am disposing myself to watch tv!'

   Now before you say disposing? Yep I know, Jake has a habit of getting his words muddled up. For example when my mother said to him;
'That's a lovely gold coin you got there, is that Egypt on the front?'
He answered; 'Yes its me Egpit one!'
 Its just Jakes colourful language, albeit it Romany or the Queens English!
   He milked that swollen nose big time. And me? Well I hadn't forgotten the stupid rackli thing. So guess who had to get their own back? Yep, you got it!
But that came later!

Jake does the daftest stuff sometimes...........

   Which reminds me of the time when we went to Morocco.

                  Chapter 14

'Why are we going to Morocco?' Jake looked at me as though I had lost my mind. Because ever since I was a kid I have been glued to the TV when anything about North Africa came on.
I promised myself then that the first time I would go abroad would be to Morocco.

 'Just think, turbans, fez's, multi coloured costumes and the Souks! I can't wait!'
'Wos' a souk mum?'
My son was shoving clothes, toys teddies and, I noticed, my best hairdryer which won't work there and its brand new and....

'No, not that one!' Grabbing the dryer I shoved it back in the drawer.
'A souk is a market or bazaar. And then of course there is the mysterious Medina, the ancient walled in town which is part of Tangiers, I can't wait to see it!'

My son looked bemused. 'But is there a beach so that I can go play there?'

'Yes of course there is!' I leaned down and brushed his hair across his forehead. 'And there's lots of shops and amazing things to see!'

'Okay' He said, and headed for the stairs, 'Gotta take my game though.'

'Not too much! We won't be able to get on the plane!'

The next day we made our way to the airport, and soon we were in departures.

'Mum can I have a drink?'
'Yes, but we have to hurry or we will miss the plane.'

I grabbed my purse and headed for one of the shops in the airport.

Jake was mooching around with a look of, what? On his face.

'Jake? You alright?'
'Not really, never been on a plane before,' he mumbled.

'Oh you'll be fine,' I said with a quick Hail Mary just in case!
'What's there to be scared of?'
Jake just shrugged.
'I hate heights!'
Oh great! I thought.
Soon it was time to board, so I grabbed my son, a carry on case and Jake.
My son was willing, the case was light and Jake? Well Jake dragged his heels so badly I literally had to carry him on board.
When we eventually got to our seats after a rather strange walk through a bendy tunnel, Jake turned to me and said, 'I wanna get off. Don't like it. It ain't natural to fly up there with them birds.'

He snuggled down into the seat looking miserable.
'You'll be fine.' I whispered and squeezed his hand.
The engines suddenly roared, and Jake roared too!
'Ahhh get me off, I don't like it!'
But of course by this time it was too late.
Clutching hold of his seat he sat forward and peered out of the window.
'Bloody 'ell! That was quick, look Nell!'
Grabbing me by the shoulder, he made me look out of the window.
By this time we were pretty high up. The clouds were just above us, and as we looked, the plane gently cut through the white and for a second it looked like fog surrounded us.
Then like an arrow heading for the sky, the plane came out on the other side.
And there, above us was blue sky and a yellow sun.
Warmth came in the window, and light lit up Jakes face. Open mouth and eyes shining.
'Wow! Look at that Nell, its bloody amazing!'
I smiled. Jake would be fine.
In fact he spent the next couple of hours muttering and exclaiming 'Oh wow, bloody hell, that's cool!' and so on.

Luckily the flight went without any mishaps and we landed at Tangiers airport at 6am.
With one exhausted boy and Jake still looking green as an unripe berry, we headed of to our hotel.
The flight had been early evening, but what with transfers, coaches and finding the right hotel it was early morning and we were shattered.

The first thing you notice when landing in a foreign country is the smell. Morocco smelled like warm apples and sand. It was also quite windy.
Reaching the hotel we were escorted to our rooms and we hit the sack with exhaustion.

But tiredness didn't keep me down for long as excitement, my son, and 'Need a drink' Jake woke me up, which left me feeling really fuzzy.
It didn't last long. I was wide awake by the time we went downstairs.

The hotel was pretty standard, but as we walked out the glass front doors, the difference hit us like a hammer. Wow!
It was so different and exotic!
The atmosphere was spices and perfumes. And when we went for a walk it was like we were awake for the first time ever.

Every sense exploded.
The light was so bright, the sky really blue. Women flitted around in bright coloured burkha's. At this time it was traditional for the women to wear these. Later on many started wearing western clothing. This was the late 80's and so different from anything I had seen before.

It was the smell that was so different from home.
Just within a few hundred metres the smell changed. Some odours were gorgeous spices, others the smell of cooking.
Walking past the leather open air shops and markets we got a tang of leather as the sun warmed the jackets and belts.

Then, around the corner right in the middle of the market stood the open air meat vendors.
They left a taste of copper and blood on our tongues.
Hanging from the hooks were many animal carcasses, most of them I couldn't recognise from a distance.
Not an unpleasant smell but we were glad to get to a cafe' and have a coffee.

One of the worse parts of being in a crowded boiling hot town is the smell of the drains.
It hit you like a wall of stink when you turned a corner, or headed along the main road. But we soon got used to it. In fact in a strange way all the smells, tastes and colours made us feel so alive!

'When we going to the beach mum?' My son was getting impatient with us just strolling around.

I looked at Jake. 'You up for the beach?'

'Go on then but we will have to get the free car down to it.' And he went of to hail the taxi.

We were quite a way from the seafront so our hotel kindly gave everyone a lift everyday.

Jumping in the car my son was so excited! It took about three minutes to get there, but what with the traffic we would have got lost, so were grateful for the lift.
'Wow!' My son took one look at the sea and off he went.

'Be careful!', I cried, 'Watch out for your feet and don't go in too far, just your ankles!'
With a grunt and a grin, he sped of across the sand.

I could hear Michael Jackson being played somewhere in the houses behind us, and it made me smile.
So much for getting away from the normal to the exotic!
Peering through my dark glasses I spotted a...
'Oh my goodness!' I sat up and shook Jake, 'Look, its a camel!'

There, coming towards us across the sand were four camels!
It was like Lawrence of Arabia. All we needed now was a hunky Arab guy on a grai riding along the side, and I would be off thank you very much!
Love ya Jake, but seeya later!

But no. The camels were drawn by four young lads wearing jeans and T shirts.
'Camel rides, camel rides!' The young man yelled out.

I couldn't get there fast enough!
'Come on Jake, Dan, where's Dan?' I yelled to him and he came skittering up the beach.

'Want a ride on a camel?'

The grin on his face said it all and before I could say wait, he was already being helped up by the smiling young man.
I climbed up behind him and Jake went on the other one.
Now if you have never been on a camel its an experience I can tell ya!

First of all you lean backwards as it gets up, then you're suddenly thrust forward as its hind legs stand.

'Whoa!' I said and nearly fell off. But I grabbed the pommel on the saddle and we were away!
Shrieking with laughter, I desperately hung on.

The motion was really quite weird, and very soothing. After a while, I could have nodded off really quickly if my camel hadn't decided to mate with Jakes!
Yep not lying!

'Help!' The young man quickly took control and I looked across at Jake.
'Typical!' I said glaring at him but laughing too. 'Trust your camel to do that!'
Jake burst out laughing and grinned all over his face.
At last! He was enjoying himself!
We went up and down the beach jogging side to side. The sun beat down and I felt like a queen!

But soon we got down, paid the few dirham's for our ride, and headed off for something to eat.

It started to get dark and we were all exhausted, so we headed back to the hotel. Hot, tired sunburned but totally relaxed. What a day!

We hit the beds running!

The next morning we were woken by the sound of the muezzin calling the faithful to prayers.
It was an amazing sound and totally alien to us westerners.
Then it was spoiled by that bloody cockerel that we came to hate after a few days! Cockadoodledooooooooo!
'Piss off!,' I yelled and grabbed the pillow and shoved my head under it. Five in the morning, bloody hell!

I had nightmares about that bloody thing for weeks!

But it was the start of our first day proper, and we headed down to breakfast.
I noticed that the hotel had filled up during the night. There were lots of local people in a huge party over by the back wall of the restaurant.
They waved and smiled. We waved and smiled back.

We never thought anything of it at the time and soon headed down to the beach and then shopping, but later that day we could hear music as we headed back to the hotel.

'Sounds good, wonder what that is?' I said.
'Dunno, hope they don't make row all night, I am shattered!' Said my wonderfully cheerful hubby Jake.
You can take him to water, but you can't make him drink!
We stepped into the cool of the lobby, crossed the floor and walked out into the sunlight.

The sound got louder as we climbed the outdoor steps to our balcony on the third floor.

There was a low wall to my right.
I stopped climbing and leaned over to take a look.
'Hey Jake come and see, Dan, where are you?'
My son climbed up next to me on a small table near the wall.
Grabbing his belt to keep him safe, we both leaned over and took in the sight.

'What they doin' mum?'
'Not sure sweetie, I think it must be a party.'

There below us, a party was in full swing. At least 30 people were dancing and the music was playing.

It was a traditional Moroccan event. There seemed to be a lot of guitar music, and women wailing.

and the clothing was a multi coloured feast of blues and reds, orange and green. Gorgeous!

'I think it must be a wedding party,' Jake said as he passed us by on the stairs.

We didn't notice another guest heading down towards us, and he overheard what we had said.
The dark haired man smiled at us and came over to where we were standing.
His voice sounded local. I was getting used to the accent.
He reached over the wall and looked down.
 'Yes its a relative of mine and his wife to be. Why don't you join us tomorrow evening for the wedding down there?' And he pointed down to the revellers.
'Oh we can't impose,' I started.

'No, its no imposition, we are Moroccan gypsies, its our tradition to invite guests to the wedding and after party.'

I looked across at Jake and smiled as he answered,
'That's really kind of you, shall we go?' He turned to me, a question on his face.

I smiled and answered, 'I would love to!'
Thanking the man we walked up the rest of the stairs to our room.
Jake had a huge grin on his face by this time.
'Gypsies! Well how about that!'

'That's really kind of them to ask us, it will be amazing! Of to bed now Dan, no, don't moan.'
I saw the look on his face. 'Yes you can read for a while.'

Grabbing his book he dived into bed.

I was looking forward to tomorrow. Little did I know what was in store!

   The day started bright and early, the sun was shining, so we decided to go straight to the beach.
The great thing about Tangiers is the breeze. The heat was boiling, but we kept cool because of the wind that constantly blew across the sands.

After a couple of hours sunbathing, eating ice cream, and jumping in the sea, we decided it was time for lunch.
Soon after, we headed back to the hotel. Me with my face the colour of mahogany and a pure white body.
My son pure cream white because I was scared to death of skin burn, so hence a whole tube of sun cream, and Jake, typically burned brown as a berry.

   When we got back the wedding was in full swing so we ran upstairs to get washed and changed.

'Mum, can I take Ted?'
'No, you'll lose him,' I said desperately searching for my purse.
'On top of that he doesn't want to go to a party, he needs his sleep!'
Fingers crossed behind my back I smiled at my son. Please don't let him take it. If we lose it there will be hell to pay.

'Jake, where are you? Jake?' Hearing a noise from the bathroom I headed that way.
'What are you doing for goodness sake its nearly time to go down!'

Snatching his tie from between his fumbling fingers, I quickly tied it for him. 'You look nice,' I noticed that he was wearing a lovely pure white suit.

'Thanks, that's the only one I got, I don't wanna look a right dinlo do I?'
He turned to look in the mirror.
'Do I look okay?'
'Yes you look great!' I kissed him.
'Come on, and Dan, move!'

Diving out the door, we all traipsed downstairs into the middle of a melee.
People were rushing everywhere, waiters were carrying trays full of local dishes, and bar staff were juggling drinks and showing off their skills.

I could see the bride. She looked amazing in her white wedding dress trimmed with gold filigree, sleeves that covered her hands, and a gorgeous thin gold chain around her forehead.

I couldn't see the groom but he was off somewhere else probably getting ready.

Funnily enough Jake had disappeared to.
But I wasn't worried. He had probably headed over for a drink at one of the bars.
But after a while I turned to my son and said 'Dan, have you seen your father anywhere?'
'Yeah,' he said, scoffing a small dainty pastry that one of the waiters and given him.
'Where is he?'
'He went off with those men.' And pointing with a sticky finger he waved in the direction of the main hallway.

Strange! He doesn't know anybody here. I thought.
Soon the music started and you could feel the hum of excitement as people shifted in their seats and turned to look at the groom.

There!

Hang on a minute.........!

'Jake? What the hell are you doing....Jake?'
I shot to my feet and ran across to where four men were propelling my struggling swearing husband towards the bride standing at the garden altar!

'Will you get the fuck off me!' Jake yelled and pulled away. He straightened his tie, fixed his jacket and glared at all and sundry!

'Do I look like the bloody bridegroom?'

Well, I just stood there gaping. My mouth wide open, catching flies as my ma would say!

What the fuck?

Eventually my feet worked against the surprise and I stormed over to confront the group of men standing around waving their arms about and all talking at once.

Seeing me come stomping over, they all turned as one, looking like a flock of demented penguins in their suits.

I stood there. Hands on hips. Feet wide apart. Ready for battle.

'Will someone please tell me what the hell is going on?'

A small swarthy man stepped forward. He was wearing a dark shirt with patterns on, and white trousers.

'I am sorry Madam....but we thought he was the bride groom! It wasn't our fault he....um, how you say? Was wearing our wedding attire, and what with his er, dark hair and skin we thought he was Moroccan!'

I just stared. I mean what was I supposed to do?

'You don't know who is getting married?' I shook my head in disbelief.

'Er, ah no Madam, we are from another City, we only know a few people's. Your husband.' at this he glared at Jake, 'Came down the stairs that are set aside for the bride and groom and....'

'I only went to the damn toilet,' Jake yelled and stepped towards the man ready to punch him on the nose!

'Jake..!'
I stepped forward and thought, 'Oh no here we go!'

'But you are wearing a white suit sir!'
Said the little man, all apologies and sweaty hands. Waving his arms around and opening and shutting his mouth like a fish.

Okay, time to take over.

'Come on Jake, sit down, have a drink and for goodness sake,' I hissed, 'Shut the hell up and let the poor bride and groom get married before we find ourselves out on the street!'
Jake looked at me, stared at the little man, huffed, puffed, then walked off.
 All I could hear was 'Dawdy what a stupid divio dinlo...crazy mother fu.....'
'Jake!' I yelled!
Scratching my head I muttered under my breath.
'Maybe I should have left him for the poor bride to sort out, at least I would get a bit of peace and quiet for a while!'

All I could hear when I went back to my seat was my son chuckling away to himself.

'He nearly got married mum, how funny!'
His giggle got louder and louder till everyone was looking at him. I smiled. We aim to please!

The rest of the evening went really well, with me teasing Jake mercilessly about marrying him off to a Moroccan gypsy bride.

But part of me was a bit, well, miffed to say the least. She was pretty. In fact very pretty and a part of me thought, what if he did prefer her?

'Oh don't be stupid woman,' I berated myself. 'he married you, so shut up.'

But I did feel better when he said later on in the day, 'It took me long enough marrying you let alone another woman! I would have run a mile!'
I smiled.
Of course that wasn't the end of it.

We were teased mercilessly by the bar staff and concierge for days after that but it was funny so we took it all in good humour.

 Of course that wasn't the only incident. Oh no.
Not with Jake around!
You see, the one thing about being on vacation in Morocco is the fact that there are lots of power cuts. At least back in the late 1980's.

We were walking down the main staircase when all of a sudden we were plunged into darkness.
'Mum!'
My son started to panic, so grabbing his hand I said, 'Its okay, I got you.'

Once again Jake did his famous disappearing act, but we weren't worried. We were in the hotel weren't we? What could possibly go wrong this time?

Suddenly we noticed a soft glowing light bobbing up the stairs. It was a man carrying a candle. Thank goodness for that! We thought.
 Looking closer we could see it was an Arab guy wearing full regalia.

A turban was wrapped around his head, and he had a long gown that draped around his ankles.
As he got closer I realised that he looked really familiar.......

'Its me! thought you might need a light!' and there, in the candle light stood Jake looking like Wee Willy Winkle!

'What the.....?'
'Yeah great ennit? I got it off the souk down the road while you lot were 'avin a kip!'

'Oh dear lord.......!'
'But its Egyptian!' I was gob smacked! 'In case you haven't noticed we happen to be miles away, in Morocco! They only wear Fez here! You look a right prat!'

There he was, on the stair, holding a candle with a look of complete pleasure on his face.
'Na, its great! They said I looked good!' Then he burst out laughing. 'Got ya there didn't I!'

I just shook my head, grabbed my sons hand and carried on walking down the stairs. I must admit I was trying not to laugh.
At the same time I tried getting as much space between us so nobody would think we were together!

He was so embarrassing sometimes!

The holiday was soon over and we got home tired, broke but sun burned. A lot. Especially me. My face looked like an old leather book that had been tanned and my son was so pale because of all the cream I had slapped on him, that he may as well had a week in Blackpool!

Jake on the other hand was dark and sexy. Bloody typical! And he hated sunbathing!
  But it was back to work, me. Back to school Dan, and back to bed Jake!
'How long you planning on staying there?' I said, hands on hips staring down at the slumbering heap wrapped up in the covers.

'When I wanna ger up I'll ger up, stop nagging me like an old dried up rackli!'
  Oh that deserved a kick in a delicate place if ever there was one!
'Oy!' I pulled the covers off the bed and threw them on the floor. Then with one almighty lunge I sprang on top of him.

'What was that you called me?'
'Ouch gerrof me ya silly cow!' Jake burst out laughing and tried pushing me off the bed.

'No, you get up or I will stay here and taunt you all day!'
'Kay! I get the point I am getting up! Anyway there's something I got to do today!' He said, and headed off to the bathroom.

'Not one of his stupid ideas I hope!' scratching my head, I grabbed my coat and headed out the door.

Now the trouble is, when Jake says he has got something to do, I know darn well that its going to involve choring. In plain English, choring is a kind of, um....borrowing?! Yep let's put it that way, nicely! Borrowing!

To be fair, they don't chor good stuff. Only old bits of copper wire, bikes that have been dumped and maybe a few other things that have been left lying around!

In fact the gypsies come in handy sometimes because they go and collect the broken metal that people dump in their gardens.
Later that day Jake turned up with an old bicycle frame and sat on the step happily stripping it down before painting it and selling it on.

Now at this point I think its time to clear up a few assumptions about gypsies.
You know the old old story. On the news, 'Gypsies have taken over an old car park and left rubbish' and
'Them bloody gypos have gone and done it again, robbed that old lady!'

Well let me tell you something. Its completely false.

To begin with, how many people know the difference between a gypsy, gorgi, traveller and didikoi?
No? Didn't think so!

Okay, now for a bedroom story kids, pull up a chair, get a coffee and sit quietly.

Chapter 15

Romany gypsies originated in the north west region of India. Surprised?
Most people believe it was Egypt but that was a fallacy.
Evidently someone nicknamed them gypsy because they had travelled through that country. And the name stuck.
 They entered Europe in the centuries between 6AD and 11AD.
 Many came to work, others arrived as slaves before being set free to return home.
 At that time there was a lot of turmoil in Europe and the Middle East. Better known as The Holy Wars between Christianity and Islam.
There were also other local wars and conflicts going on at this time.

 Many Romanies headed east and settled in all the European Capitals. And many came to Britain.
They brought their own colourful culture and lifestyle.
Over the years they have tried to keep those traditions alive as much as possible.
 In all that time, gypsies have contributed to our way of life. Most gypsy families helped out with hop picking, gathering strawberries and other fruits and generally finding work on the land. This is how they earned their living and provided for their families.

 Their cleverly made pots and pans were eagerly bought by many a household, and wives and mothers from gorgie families were happy to buy their bright coloured pegs that were handmade.
You could always tell when the gypsies had passed through a village.
Every house had sprigs of lavender or holly outside their doors, and inside on the window ledge were beautiful flowers picked by gypsy women.

 For many years right up until the 1960's people got excited to see the multi coloured vardo's heading into their towns.
But then something happened.
The law began to change. Gypsies were not allowed to park their caravans and vardo's on public land.
Hop picking and other jobs on the land were becoming mechanised.
 Soon the gypsy way of life began to change. And with this change began suspicion and hate.
Soon it became normal to see a police car appear the second that the gypsies parked up.
Being constantly moved on became the norm.

 Soon many Irish Travellers began to arrive in England and this caused more dissent.
Travellers and gypsies have a long history of animosity between them. And this didn't help the fact that the police and those in authority decided to bunch gypsies and travellers together and call them by the collective name, Gypo's!

Obviously politic correctness didn't reach as far as our ancient friends the Romany Gypsies! And it seems that it still doesn't today.
 If there is one thing that both gypsies and Irish travellers hate being called is dirty. Both have their ways of living, and both are probably cleaner than the average 'normal' person.

The ones who leave a mess, broken gates, tons of rubbish and so on, do not belong to the 90% of the Romany/Traveller community who cringe in dismay and disgust at seeing this happen.

 If you ever have the chance to go into a real gypsy caravan you will be surprised at just how spotless it is.
Gold rimmed cups and saucers. Thick floor rugs. Snow white bedding and lovely clean walls and windows.
Outside their caravans are beautiful gardens with statues and ponds. And the Travellers are the same.

 The Irish travellers are not Romany gypsies. Their bloodline is pure Irish.
Their language is predominantly Shelta and Irish Traveller Cant.
There is a lot of speculation about the origin of Irish Travellers in the sense of when they started out.
Some say they worked for Romany gypsies, and then split off on into their own groups.
Genetics on the other hand say that many Irish moved away from the main group over a thousand years ago.
 Either way, they are not the same blood line as Romany gypsies.
And this is where the problems start. Some of the Irish Traveller traditions are totally different to Romany.
For example, Traveller men teach their sons to fight from an early age.

This can cause all sorts of trouble with the local population who think they are deliberately causing hassle.

And of course there is the rubbish they leave behind when they vacate their site.
To be fair gypsies can be messy too, but in the case of the 'rubbish wars' its usually the Travellers.
 Or Travellers who have set up on their own. And lets face it, they probably do it deliberately to annoy the gorgi's!
Saying that, the majority of Gypsy folk and Travellers, are very nice clean people.

But you can't tell that to us gorgi's.

 As for Diddikai's(didicoy, diddicoy), These are the children of gypsies who marry a gorgi. Not like the original meaning.
Over the years the word Dikkikai has changed from full blooded gypsy to mixed blood.

Here's a perfect example in this old well known gypsy song written by C Bellamy and G Weeks in 1885.

The song has been changed so many times over the years, but this version is believed to be the original.

It started out as a poem. Over the years gypsies would tell it round the camp fire.

If you have never sat and listened to gypsies singing either in a public place or traditionally outside their Vardo's, its a sight to see.

The women dance or tap in time to the music and the men raise their voices, not always in tune but the melodies that come out are wonderful.

Here's an example:

I'm a Romano Rai, just an old didikai,
I build all my temples beneath the blue sky,
I live in a tent and I don't pay no rent,
and that's why they call me the Romano Rai.
Didi-a-didi-a-didi-di-kai, chavves,
Tika-dika-tika-a-lai, (or can be; Kakka Chavve, Dekh akai)

Your Daddus tryin' to sell a mush a kushto grai.

But that's why they call me the Romano Rai.

I'm a Romano rai, just an old didikai,
I live in a mansion beneath the blue sky,
I was born in a ditch, so I won't ever grow rich,

Tikka, tikka, didikai, tikka, tikka, didikai
That's why they call him the Romano Rai.

Tikka-tikka-didikai, tikka tikka, didikai,
That's why they call him the Romani Rai.

I'm a Romano Rai, a true didikai,
My temple's a mansion beneath the blue sky,
I'm a Romano Rai, a true didikai,
just campin' around, on any ol' ground,

But that's why they call him the Romano Rai.

-

I believe this is how many people see traditional gypsies. Sitting around a vardo singing and dancing.

And in fact back in the 50's and 60's many Vardo's were seen trotting gently along the road with their grai's (horses) pulling them from village to village.

It was a hard life, but back then there was a certain rhythm to their lives. Part of the the year they would all head towards work that would keep the whole family busy for a few weeks.
  At first it would be hop picking, then the first flowers of spring would bud and the women would make them into small bunches to be sold in towns.
Then they would move on to other towns and join different relatives.
  They would meet up at least twice a year with their families.
  Family gatherings would bring in other gypsies from around the countryside. This would be a great opportunity for meeting and greeting, and especially for parents to find a suitable husband for their daughters.

  Its only in modern times that girls are allowed to pick their husbands, but there are still certain traditions and expectations to be had before the rings are exchanged and vows are taken.
It definitely wouldn't have been the 'done thing' for gorgies like me to marry into a Romany family.
They would have both been outcasts and likely to have ended up living as a house dweller!

  I first met Jake when I was working and didn't for a second think that he was a gypsy. It was one hell of a shock to my mother! As I mentioned before, she wasn't a very happy woman!

But over the years she warmed to him, and before she died she really did appreciate everything he did.
I on the other hand, have always been a bit wary of his family!

  Jake comes from a family of six children. He is the second eldest. And when I met the rest of the family I wasn't sure what to think.
I was used to a warm happy atmosphere at home. This didn't feel the same.

In fact, I felt it the moment I walked into their living room.
  Jakes mother was really sweet giving me cups of tea and biscuits, and asking if I needed anything.
 His older sister rushed around taking my coat and getting all in a fluster.
  But there was an atmosphere. I could feel it, and when the back door opened there was a change in the air.

  In the doorway appeared a dark haired man with swarthy features. When my mother saw him later she exclaimed. 'He only needs a caravan and horse, you can see what he is!'

And yes he was a typical Romany. But there was an air about him, and I wasn't sure how to proceed.

There was a huge scramble for the door as all the family ran to make sure he was comfortable.
Jakes sister picked up his slippers.
His wife shot out to the kitchen and grabbed his dinner quickly, opening the knife draw and taking out the cutlery.
And Jake sat forward on his chair waiting for the bomb to drop!
Me? I just sat there feeling completely uncomfortable.

So this was what it was like to be part of a gypsy family.
But later I found out that wasn't necessarily so. Not all gypsy fathers were so, well, intimidating!

Father came first. In every part of their lives, he was the boss. And he was always right. Well, according to him anyway.
   I never really got on with him, purely because he presumed over the next few years that I would be a typical gypsy wife.
Do this, do that, and so on.
But I am not like that. Oh no. I am a gorgi woman totally independent. So you can see why we bumped heads!

  At this first meeting he sat down and stared at me.
'Who's this then?'
When he was told I was dating his son he laughed. 'Ah that won't last long then!'
Thirty years later......but I digress.
Talk about cut the air with a knife!
I had never met anyone like him before. I knew Jake was wary of him for good reason. But that's another story, and not mine to tell.
I did try to get on with them. But the kids had all learned to be self reliant. Don't trust anyone, especially an outsider.
But time goes on, and we did visit them once a week. I loved his mum. And she adored my son.
That was enough.
Sadly Jakes mother died at an early age, and his father passed away ten years ago.

  It wasn't all bad, and I was sad to see him go.
I know the rest of his family still mourn him very much.
These past years we have all mellowed, and I now get on with his brothers and sisters, which is a blessing.
It seems that, with the patriarch of the family no longer with us, hearts have softened and I have warmed to them. Even visiting frequently and laughing hard together. Great times.

Chapter 16

It was hard work bringing up a child, Jake trying desperately to get a job and maintaining a caravan with no main drainage.
Just dragging huge water bottles up and down the site was a pain in the backside.

And of course trying to keep the caravan clear of leaks or mould.
That's the trouble living in a tin can!

It was freezing cold in the winter, and the hot summer days were like living in an oven, gas mark 350!

When we arrived back from our vacation it was Autumn which is the Goldie locks month.
Not too hot, not too cold.
But I knew the days were drawing in, so I had to start sorting out our winter clothes, making sure light bulbs were in order and checking that our gas bottles were up to date and full.
Talking about gas bottles.......!

'Where are you going Jake?' I asked one day a few weeks later.
It was a cold snow covered night in the middle of winter, with three foot of the white stuff outside our door.
Looking rather sheepish Jake replied, 'You know that shop through the park, the one that sells gas bottles and water tanks?'
'Here we go' I thought.
'Well,' He grinned ' Did you know it was empty now?'
'Sooooo....' I said.
'Well I think he's left a few empty bottles around the back!'
'Great' I flinched.
Empty water bottles and boilers were huge. They would fetch a fortune in scrap metal.....
Oh no he wasn't expecting me to go traipsing through three foot of snow to help him, was he?

Luckily he decided he didn't need me. Pulling on his coat and gloves he headed out the door. I followed him and watched in amusement as he crept over the white snow and headed into the park.
Hold on a minute! Why is he sneaking around if the shop is closed and.....!
'Oh no!' I thought, scrambling for my coat. Then I decided against it. If Jake was up to no good then I didn't want to be associated with it.
So I waited. And I waited. And waited.
Till finally after two long hours.......
I was beginning to panic. Where the hell was he?
I peered out of the window. The snow was falling in thick sheets of white and I couldn't see a thing. Yet....
There!
Suddenly out of the white I saw a figure rush by on the road!

'What the hell was that?' I thought.
It looked like some kind of deformed monster! Big head, little arms, no neck!
Two seconds later, after he or it had disappeared, I saw another man rush round the corner screaming his head off!
'Oh Lord!' I thought and ducked down inside underneath the window. Don't twitch the curtains don't......! My brain was doing all sorts of crazy things. Do I go out? Or should I stay in?
Next second the answer became clear.

'Come back 'ere you thievin' bastard! Come back!'
'Oh shit with sugar and dumplings on it! What the hell had Jake done?'
Checking on my son to make sure all the hoo ha hadn't woken him, I opened the front door just in time to see Jake rush past the other way carrying a very heavy water tank. And in his wake a very irate fat guy who by this time was blue in the face and waving his arms around his head like some sort of Viking berserker!
My blood ran cold. Well I was cold already, bloody freezing in fact!
I hissed at Jake.
'Jake, Jake for Christ's sake, what the bloody hell are you doing?'
Then the hiss turned into a yell!

 'JAKE COME INSIDE AND STOP MAKING AN ARSE OF YOURSELF!'
But there was one problem. Jake couldn't come in because he had a maniac chasing him!
I had to cause a distraction, but what could I do?
I spotted the old bike outside. Ha! that will do it.
it was a small trike, and without thinking about what I was doing, I picked it up and swung it with all my strength and lobbed it at the yelling man!
I didn't want to hurt him, just distract him!
But.......!
I misjudged the angle and to my horror, it fell straight in front of him.
He saw it.
Too late!
His arms started flaying about, his body pitched forward and to this day I can't think of it without laughing.
There he was, sitting half on the snow and the rest of his bulk on the collapsed bike trying to get up while yelling and swearing!
Oops!
A fat man, draped round a red bike in the white snow. Not something you easily forget!
Of course he couldn't get up because it was slippery with ice. A few cars slid past but nobody stopped to help him.
The street lights flickered and for a few seconds the muffled silence of a snowy cold winters night descended on the scene.
I took a deep cold breath and wondered what to do.
I would have offered to help him but.....!

   He just lay there swearing and cussing.
Jake by this time had legged it round the back of the caravan and I was left standing there, mouth agape, like a rabbit caught in the headlights.

'Um' I gulped. 'Can I help you?'
'What did you do that for?' The man yelled.
'I um, thought you were a burglar trying to mug someone, I was only trying to help!'
I stared wide eyed. Trying to use all my charm.
And my skimpy nightdress didn't hurt either! Did I forget to mention the fact that I was getting ready for bed?
He peered up at me. 'Can you give me a lift up? That son of a bitch just stole a copper boiler off me!'
I noticed when he got indignant his double chin wobbled like a jelly on a plate.
'Interesting' I thought, then stifled a laugh.
'Well are you going to help me?'
'Er sorry, I can't come out I am not dressed, but would you like me to call the police?' I asked all innocent, fingers crossed behind my back.
'No forget it, he's got away now' he said crossly.
He staggered to his feet and then turned to me.
'Did you see which way he went?' He asked.
'No, I only saw you chasing a monster man!' No I never said that, but I wish I had!
Instead I said, 'No, he was too fast for me to see where he went.'

Coward. Yes I know what your thinking. Your getting as bad as him, blah blah. But tell me, what was I supposed to do? Let him in? Make him a cuppa tea while Jake was staggering around the back of the Vardo like a demented frozen robot? So no. instead......
'I hope you get home okay, and if you need anything please don't be scared to knock on my door, okay?'
brushing himself down he stood for a moment looking up at the night sky.
'I don't know, what is it with folks these days?'
He turned and walked away.
I was mortified.

I went back inside and there on the chair was Jake!
'How did you.....?'
Seeing my face, he started laughing. 'Get us a cuppa char will ya? I'm knackered!'
I just stared. Then all my senses snapped on at once.

'You said it was an empty shop! You said it was a doddle, easy bloody peasy! What the hell happened?'
I stormed across the room and glared full toxic glare at Jake.
He shifted in the chair. Trying to look humble he raised his eyebrows and said 'He came back to get somethin,' spotted me round the back wiv the water tank on me back and I scared the crap outta him!'
He sniffed and smirked.
'Don't you smirk at me!,' I stormed. 'What happened then?'
'Well....,' He let the sound out like a slow whistle.
'I just grinned and legged it!' laughing he lunged at me and said, 'giss a kiss, I'm cold!'
Then he pulled a face.
That was Jake, always trying to get round me.
But it didn't wash with me!

I took a swipe at him, but he ducked.
He laughed, whistled and headed for the bedroom.
'Night my love, goin' ta bed, knackered!'
And he was gone.
So there I was aiding and abetting a thief and all he could say was....
'Lovely bit o' tott, this is going to get me at least 30 quid.' He scratched his head as he yelled back over his shoulder.
'Where's me cuppa?'
'Umph!' I said, and turned, heading for the bedroom.
'Get it yourself!'

The next day I wrote a small note, and added 20 quid. Putting it in an envelope I walked across the park and put it gently through the shop door. I could see someone in the back so I hurried across the grass and home.
Jake may think its okay, but I am a gorgie and proud. Some things were just not on.

That was the final time Jake did anything like that.
Well, as far as I know!

To be fair, he really did think it was an empty shop. I got chatting to the ex owner one day while doing my shopping down town. He said the firm had gone broke and he was sick and tired of selling water buckets and, I quote:
'Damn bloody gas bottles that stink the God damn place out!'
And was quite happy with his retirement. I never told him who I was, and never mentioned our 'slight indiscretion. So, it seemed that all was well! Phew!

Chapter 17

Jake wasn't always the cleverest tool in the box, if you know what I mean! Sometimes he got things wrong. But on the whole he was a generous guy who loved kids, animals and, well you get my point!

Talking of kids, he was often seen out the front of our caravan chatting to the parents, playing footie with the boys and throwing the babies up in the air. I think it was his child like sense of fun that made them love him.
Summer nights were particularly fun. Whole families would congregate in the road that circled the site, and we would all get together and play games, have a drink or just a sing song.
As I said to Jake, 'You can take the travelling out of a gypsy but you would never change his soul.'

Of course there were fights. And boy were they humdingers!
I remember one time in particular. Luckily Jake had gone out so he was away from the trouble. But the whole caravan site must have heard this one!

Two guys, both from the same family had decided to get together after not speaking for years. I learned all this in the aftermath!
Evidently one of them made the mistake of saying;
'Ya well ya Mrs aint no oil painting is she?'
Before he had a chance to say he was only joking, well I think he was.....there was a god all mighty thump and they were off!
Of course we all had to go and check it out being good neighbours and all!

My son was with his dad, so I locked up the vardo and headed down the road and round the corner.
I could see faces at all the windows, and the doors were beginning to open.
'What the hell is goin' on?' a young lad sat on the wall scratching his head.

'I don't know Levi, but if ya don't git out my way I'll shove ya out the way!' said a small boy with black hair and a freckled face.

As I neared the fracas I saw that someone had set up a chair and bench.
So It was going to be a long night with lots of fisticuffs, blood and possibly hangovers in the morning!
'S'cuse me,' I said as I tried to get round the edge of the circle that had congregated outside the caravan.

Spotting old Vic sitting on his caravan steps smoking a roll up, I made my way over.
'Hiya Vic, what's up?' I said indicating the crowd.
Vic was slow and old. He took the cigarette out of his mouth blew a cloud of smoke into the air and then sighed.
'Ain't sure yet m'dear but it looks like its gonna be nasty!' He said this last with relish!
With a gleam in his eye he shifted over on the step and offered me a seat.
'Cigarette missy?'
'Thanks.' I said and waited while he made me a rolly.

'The trouble with the chavi's these days, is that they got the beng In em!'
And it did indeed seem as though they had the devil in them.
The two men were circling each other, ready to take a punch. One, tall dark haired and scruffy, was muttering under his breath.
'I'm gonna kill ya for talkin' like that about ma woman!'
The other man was smaller but looked more compact. If I had to place bets I would put him down as the winner.
He wasn't saying anything, but a look of concentration on his face spoke volumes.
Suddenly old Vic stood up on the step and yelled:
'Kel the bosh. Kel the bosh.'
Kel the what...?

Next second the violin, fiddle? Was brought out and the air was struck with sweet colourful music. Someone piped up with;
'Chaunt Sara, go on, give us a song.'

And there, in the middle of the caravan site, a young girl no older than 14 or 15 started to sing.
Her voice was high and sweet. As she sang her skirt swirled around her legs, and as the light from the caravans spilled onto her face, it gave her an angelic glow.
As the fight became more heated, the more the violin played louder and the singing became sweeter.
I was struck by a weird sense of time.

The music, the fighting and the light seemed to blend into one and for just a second, it was a hundred years ago.
The light on the singers face was from a bonfire. The music was being played by a gypsy king. The caravans took on the shape of old wooden vardo's gleaming in the moon light. Smoke from cigarettes blended with the smell of blood and perfume. I was entranced.

Then the spell was broken by Vic giving me a shove.
'You look like you're enjoying this!' He laughed and coughed.
I smiled. The reality was much more stark. By now the fighting was calming down. Both men were exhausted. I wasn't sure if it was the fight or the atmosphere that had totally knackered them. And I wasn't sure who had won. If any!

But I knew one thing. I would never forget that night.
One by one we walked back to our vans. Some carrying children, others pushing and punching each other on the shoulder and laughing.
A few were exchanging money, obviously a bet had been placed on the winner.
I took a last look over at the two fighting men.
They were hugging each other. One laughed and put out his hand. The other shook it, and they stepped back inside their caravan.
I realised at that point that I had been witness to something old and sacred.
I felt quite honoured in a strange way, to feel that I had been accepted in the group, and allowed to watch it.
  Letting myself in to my caravan, I walked across to the stove and placed the kettle on it. Not many people got to experience that sort of gathering. In a way it was amazing, in another, bloody.
Maybe there was more gypsy in me than I realised.
  I had just boiled the kettle and set out the cup when there was a knock at the door.
'Its me, open up!'
Turning I leaned over and opened it.
Huffing and puffing, Jake picked up the bags and helped our son inside.
'Did I miss anything?' He said.
'Oh yes!' I replied with a smile.

Chapter 18

One day when my son was only a few months old, he started to cough. At first it seemed like a normal cough and cold. The weather had been miserable for weeks and I put it down to being a typical child illness.
How wrong can you be?
A few days later as I was washing up in the caravan, Jake came rushing in with Dan.
'I don't want to worry ya, but there is something wrong with the babe.'
I turned around just as the baby started coughing and coughing. His face went blue and Jake seeing his distress, grabbed him out of the pushchair and turned him upside down and slapped his back.
'Oh my god! I think he needs to go to hospital!'
I panicked and ran to the door.
'Keep an eye on him while I run to the phone box and call for an ambulance!'
I don't think I have ever run so fast as I did that day. By the time I got to the phone box I was panting so hard.
'Hello? I need an ambulance my baby is choking and coughing, I don't know what to do!'
The voice on the other end had a calming influence on me and by the time I got out of the phone booth I wasn't shaking so much.

They were great. It couldn't have been more than a few minutes before I heard the ambulance racing up the road.
By this time all the neighbours had come out and were keeping us calm.
'Don't ya worry, the lil' sprog will be fine.' said Vic.
Patting me on my back.
The ambulance pulled up and two men and a woman jumped out.
'In here?' the lady pointed to my front door.
'Yes' I panted as I raced up the steps and dived indoors.
I tried seeing over the top of their backs as they checked my baby.

'I think he's got whooping cough love.' The dark haired paramedic guy said, putting away his stethoscope.
'What? Oh my god! Will he be alright?' I grabbed his sleeve.

'Don't panic love, he will be fine, but he probably needs antibiotics.' he gathered up my son in his arms and headed out the door to the ambulance.

I turned to Jake. 'What do we do? Can you bring him some clothes and other things and I will go with him to the hospital.'
Jake stood the caravan door. The look on his face was one of despair. I had never seen him look like that before.
'Don't worry,' I said, 'They said he will be fine.'
Where I was getting my strength from was anybody's guess.
The neighbours stood silently watching. A few patted me on the back and others smiled and nodded.
I smiled back, a slight quiver touching my lips.
'Please God let him be okay.' I prayed.

We arrived at the hospital and after checking him over, my baby boy was put in a seat that stood on the hospital bed. Around him they placed plastic curtains.

'This is to protect him from germs, keep him upright so that his lungs can drain, and we will then pump steam into the tent to help him breath, okay? It looks kind of strange but trust me this will make the poorly lad much better.'
The doctor smiled and touched my arm.
'There's a bed for you too, if you are planning on staying with him.'
Staying? Of course I'm staying!

We were there for nearly a week. Jake brought in all the stuff we believed was needed, which wasn't a lot as my boy was still in the tent.
But his colour had come back, and I for one was so relieved I could have cried.
'We have got to get out of that draughty mouldy caravan.' I stated.
Jake nodded. He didn't look happy about it but he knew it was the right thing to do.
'Okay, I'll see what I can do.'
I knew it would hurt him to move, but our son had to come first.
A few days later we left the hospital and I went to stay with my mum and dad.
I was there for a week, then I took my boy back home.
We asked the council if we could be moved, but they said not straight away.
So we stripped the caravan, painted the walls and made sure any holes were covered up.
Then once again I discovered that I was pregnant.

Jake was delighted, but as he said. 'We can't stop here.'
Back then in the early eighties the council was a lot harder than it is today. In other words compassion didn't come easily I discovered, where it concerned gypsies.
In plain English we didn't count for much.
I'm not sure what happened exactly but one minute I was five months pregnant, and the next I was being rushed into hospital.
I had a coil fitted which turned out to be as much use as a dog with a skirt.
At nearly six months I lost the baby.
That was a dark time. I can't remember much about it afterwards but depression hit.

I tried to forget it had happened. But of course over the years the memory comes back and hits me hard. I should have had counciling. How I coped I do not know.
But time goes on.
Soon afterwards the council gave us a brand new house. I think they felt guilty! Or maybe not.
And it was brand new. They had only just been built!
Trouble was, it sat right on the top of a hill, and the road leading to it was a one in three.
This meant that every single time me, the buggy, the baby and the shopping had to climb a huge steep hill I got asthma!
It was a nightmare living there. Winter came, and I ended up in hospital because the snow was so thick, I couldn't make it up the hill.

After collapsing again and again climbing that damn bloody hill the council changed their mind and put us in somewhere you wouldn't put a dead cat for burial!

Court Moor!
Just the name sends horrors down my back.
On the outside, it looked like old army huts. Slate roofing, low hung doors and sky high weeds that made their way through the windows and into the bedroom.
Turned out that the slate was actually made from asbestos!
One of the most deadly natural minerals that was used for all sorts of stuff until they realised just how dangerous it was.
But back then, it was par for the course.
What we didn't know was that it was meant to be a halfway house between council properties.
And the other thing that wasn't mentioned?
All the neighbours were gorgi ex offenders!
Now by this time you may notice It was an 'Us or them' situation.
I may have been born gorgi, but after living with those lovely people I suddenly had a huge dislike of normal people. Don't get me wrong, not all gorgi's. Just these offenders.
And boy did they cause trouble!
Long gone was the 'want a cuppa char?' or 'Would you like me to help you with...?'
No. These bastards stole parcels from our doorstep, caused fights and were downright pig ignorant!
Gawd did we have some fights there! Me included! There were some rough old boots living there, I can tell ya!
One in particular was horrible. We called her Queen Bee. She thought she ran the place.
She did. Till I took over! Never knew I had it in me!
She left like a scolded cat and was never seen again.

But the worse one of the lot was the bitch from hell!
She did the one thing that set my blood boiling and my temper steaming. She tried it on with my man!

We were sitting in my front room, or shit hole call it what you will, when she turned to him and put her hand on his knee.

I stopped what I was doing and waited. Now I am not the sort to go bawling out at women for trying it on with my man. Two reasons.
One, because I didn't want to give her the satisfaction, and two, I needed him to do it. That way they would know it came from the horses mouth so to speak.
On this particular day it did.
Jake blew up like Mount Vesuvias on a bad day!
'GET YOUR FUCKING HANDS OFF ME!'
I have never seen a gorgi jump so high it was like the grand national without the horse! She shot out that door like someone had stuck a red hot poker up her arse!
I looked at Jake.
He was fuming.
'Um, do you think she got the hint my love?' I asked with the most innocent look on my face. Raising my eyebrows I turned and looked at him.
Well, if a face could burn a hole in a person, his burned so bright with anger I thought It best to get some water ready to put out the flame!
Wait for it! I thought. Wait........
'Bloody stupid chickly dinlo choviar! As if I'd get near that divi rackli old joobly kennick!' he huffed and he puffed. His face about to explode.
'Well', I thought. 'That's a no then!'

I don't think I had ever seen Jake so angry! Boy was he mad!
And that wasn't the end of it.
They had it in for us then. The bitch and her Rottweiler of a husband. Seems he didn't know or maybe didn't care that his ugly fat jelly mould of a wife had tried it on with another guy.
They did everything to cause us trouble. In the end it culminated in me doing something I had never done before.
I knocked the bastard out!
He had come to the door and started a fight with Jake. It progressed to the lawn outside. Jake by this time had got him on the floor.
But I wasn't having any of it. They had made me so stressed and mad over the previous months that this time, this day and this minute zoomed into a pinpoint of white light. Anger.
Screaming white hot anger hit my body and I ran towards the bastard on the floor.
Kicking Jake out the way I lunged at Tony with my fists flaying.
'You fucking bastard!' thump, 'You make me sick! I have had two miscarriages because of you and that thick piece of trash wife of yours!' kick. 'No more! No fucking more!'
And with one final kick I smashed his face down on the floor.
Pumping breath from my body, sweat pouring down my back and forehead I stood up and over him.
Silence.
After a few minutes I looked round.
Jake was sitting on the grass, his mouth wide open. The neighbours were holding each other back, a look of horror on their faces.
I began to realise, with a sick feeling right down to my stomach, that I had been lowered to the most basest of beings.

Thanks to them. Thanks to all of them.
I wanted to get out there and then. I wanted my caravan, my friends, and my gypsy neighbours.
I was no longer gorgi.

We were there for two more bloody long years.
and then we were given a house.
But a house cannot bring back two miscarriages.
I had lost a 2nd trimester baby when living in the caravan.
Now two pregnancies at three months because of these bastards.
Some things you just can't forgive.

Chapter 19

It took Jake ages to get used to being a 'House dweller' again.
'I want to be back in a caravan!' he stomped around.
I just stood and stared.
'What?'
'You 'eard, I hate living in a bloody gorgi dwellin.'
'We will have to wait till Dan is a bit older, and the caravan has to be spotless and damp free.'
I carried on doing my washing. Folding the sheets I turned to Jake.
'Give it another year till he is five then we will go back, okay?'
Jake smiled and walking across the room hugged me to the moon and back.

So after four and a half long years of hell we ended back where we started!
Only this time it was a much bigger and better caravan. One I could live in for good.
Long story short, Jakes uncle? Cousin? Don't ask me they call every single gypsy, cousin, etc! Anyway whoever he was, we got the van cheap.
So there we were, back at the beginning, and I for one was happy with it too.
And most important? Dan was healthy and looking forward to going back to the site.
Kushti.

Days passed and we soon got back into the swing. There was old Vic still sitting on his step.
Joan living next door with her vast amount of cats. And old Sara round the way yelling out greetings through her broken front tooth. Well at 80 years old what do you expect?

Colourful curtains, the smell of clean washing flapping in the wind and old traditional music seeping out of the windows and dancing jauntily across the road.
Fun times. I was home. And it was wonderful.

The sun was shining, the grass was....Oh shit!
'Who's dog did this great big fucking....dump in my garden?'

Oh dear lord, trust Jake to break the spell.
'Don't you traipse that through my caravan!' I said, trying not to laugh.
'For fucks sake.....!'
Jake shook of his shoe and hopped around the garden.
'I'll get the hose, hang on.'
 Stepping into the caravan I grabbed the hose, and ran down the steps. Luckily we were near the main drainage tap which was situated in the road outside the van.
Turning it on, I aimed it in the right direction. Or thought I did.
'Watch what your doing you stupid......arghhhh!'
Jake was running around like a blue arsed fly trying to get away.
What was I doing?
Yep! You guessed it. I couldn't help it! I soaked him from top to bottom and nearly caused a riot with the other gypsies who were choking with laughter!

'Ay ya needed a bath ya dirty sod!'
'He's right under her thumb ain't he?'
'Go on girl give him some, ah dordi dordi what a dinlo! Give him a good soaking he's joobly!'
At that all the men laughed their heads off.

I turned to one of the girls. 'Joobly?'
With a wide grin she said, 'Lousy!' and burst out laughing!
Of course he wasn't but we did have a laugh. Jake took it in good faith, eventually!
After mumbling about gorgies, rackli's and so on he headed indoors to get dry. I think the dog shit was forgotten. Or at least I hoped it was. And not on my carpet!

 We never did find out who's dog it was! But old Vic did look a bit shifty when I asked him about it. His dog looked shifty too. A bloody big great Dane!

Chapter 20

There was great excitement round the site.

The Funfair was coming to town! This wasn't the fair that we had been to before. No this was pure blooded gypsy fairground stuff.
Once or twice a year the local Romany's got together with the showmen and fairground guys.
And bang! One hell of a big party!

I was born on Regatta day in the town where I was born.
My Mum took one look at the waltzing waltzers and went into labour!
So you could say its in my blood. Or at least my Mothers!
'Come on Jake, grab the stuff and hurry up!' I jumped the steps and landed on the grass.
'Where's Dan? Oh there he is.'
'Mum can I take my bike?'
'No.'
'But Mum.......' he stamped his foot.
'Do you want to go to the Fair or not?'
'Oh, okay then.'
He slammed the bike down and headed off down the road towards the entrance to the site.
'Wait for me.' I yelled and grabbed my handbag.
My sons mood soon lifted and we were off!

It wasn't far, so we walked and soon we could hear the tinny music wafting over the houses.
'Ooh that smell!' I sniffed, eyes closed, 'typical fairground smell of hot dogs, burgers, and candy floss, lovely!'
'Smells like horse shite to me!' holding his nose, Jake quickly crossed over the road and headed for the main gates.
'Oh crap cakes, here we go again!' I thought as we followed him in.
Jake could be a miserable bugger sometimes. His idea of the fair was working on it, not wandering around and spending money!
But I knew the second he got into the fairground he would cheer up.
And yep, there we go!
Jake was off like a greyhound after a lopping rabbit. I say lopping because I had one once. A lopping rabbit I mean. Actually its called a lop eared.
The rabbit, not Jake! Keep up!

Anyway back to the excitement.
Jake was going from stall to stall, shaking hands, his voice getting louder and louder and.....

'Yeah mate, kushti to see ya. Hows the wife, got a new chavi? That's great! Nell? Yep she's okay. She's around 'ere somewhere, Nell? Come and meet me ol' mate Billy!'
'Good to see ya love, is this your son?' turning to Dan, he held out his hand and shook my sons little fingers in his.
'Up you come lad,' and picking him up, he placed my son on one of the rides. 'don't worry, its on me!'

And it was like that for the rest of the afternoon. Dan must have had more rides than all the kids in the park.

I won a cuddly toy on the coconut shy and Jake shot enough ducks to feed an army if they had been real!
Mind you, he nearly took the stall guys eye out as he took a shot and the gun went haywire!

'Er sorry mate, you kushti?' Jake didn't know whether to look sorry or laugh.
'I'd better sit for a minute, shook me up a bit!' The young man definitely looked shaken.
'Yeah, just take a prize for the little un'.' he said.
'And go!' I muttered.
After three hot dogs, two burgers and a huge candy floss between us we were totally knackered, but it was fun tired if you know what I mean.
On the way out I turned to Jake.
'Hang on, look!' I pointed to the huge big wheel sitting in the middle of the park.
'You can fuck off!' Jake walked quickly towards the exit.
'I ain't getting on that thing! You know I hate heights!'
'Ah ha... ' I secretly sniggered.
'This is going to be fun.......!'
'Aw Jake, come on Dan doesn't want to go, and Billy said he would hold him while we went up! You don't want to look a wuss in front of Billy now do you.....?'
Got him! And he knew it!
Muttering under his breath, he was good at that, he turned, smiled and picked Dan up.
'Here you go Bill, look after me son for a minute will ya?'
And with that, he turned grabbed my hand and yelled back; 'Won't be long, the missus wants a ride on 'ere!'
Settling into the chair we pulled down the metal bar that would keep us safe. Ah! I smiled. I know its safe but Jake...?

'Alright mate?' I turned to my hubby sitting there looking like butter wouldn't melt.
Actually looking closer, I noticed that he had gone a nice shade of butter. You know the one I mean. Sort of yellowish and shiny.
'Okay?'
'Ummph.'
I take it he meant yes.
And we were away!
The seat started rising, and as we got higher and higher......
'Look Jake we can see right over the other side of the river from here!'
'Ummph!'
Well that's a start. At least he spoke. He must be getting better at this height stuff.
'And look!', I pointed 'There's your friend Molly on the ghost ride!'
Silence.
'Jake?'
Turning I looked at him. Oh. He did look kinda odd!
Suddenly he grabbed my hand.
'Let me down......now!' a whisper.

'Sorry, I can't do that, you'll have to wait till its finished.'
'Well bloody well hurry up then!'
More of a shout there. That's good. At least he's alive!
   Slowly the ride came down and Jake, with his feet touching Terra Firma, the firmer the better...managed at last to escape from the metal bar and leg it over to Billy who was holding my son in a death grip.
'You can let him go now Billy, he ain't going to escape!'

With an apologetic grin, Billy put Dan down, wiped his hand on his trousers and offered it out to Jake.
Jake shook the hand and stepped back. He still looked a bit pale, but the colour was coming back nicely.
I on the other hand was beginning to feel slightly, er, guilty for putting him through it!

'You alright mucka?' Bill leaned forward and peered into his eyes. His brows getting lower and lower as the thought that Jake was going to pass out went through his mind.

'Yep mate, I am fine. In fact I love it! Can't wait to go on it again!'
Turning to me he said with a look of...what? Annoyance? Humour? Not sure....

'But me missus is feeling a bit sick, cos she hates heights! Better get her home!'
Eyebrows raised, pursed lips I set off after him, with Dan giggling in the background.

'You bugger.....!'

   To be fair I didn't realise just how much he hated heights. He is such a strong guy, who always sticks up for himself, and his family.
That was his Achilles heel.
And we all had one of those. I never took the piss again.
A few years later when I was really sick with Graves Disease (thyroid) and I became allergic to my medication, and my bones and muscles hurt so much I could scream, he carried me from room to room. Upstairs and down, until he was exhausted. But he would never show it.

I won't ever forget that. I love him to the worlds end and back.
Simple as that.
I was lucky. So many Romany men are hardened. Not just for the continuous fights they have between one another for practice. But hard. Inside.
Oh, they love their families, but the lifestyle is such that for many of them they spend all their time trying to earn money. Or making sure the other travellers are okay.
Its a hard life, and it makes them tough.
But Jake has a soft funny side to him. When we first met all I could see was hard and wary.
He didn't trust anyone. His family life had served to show him how he had to live on his own.
I am not going to throw blame around but suffice to say Jake lived rough for a while, then ended up in a halfway house in Taunton Somerset.

It was while all this was going on I met him. Well to be fair, by the time we got together he had moved into a flat owned by an old guy and another lodger.

We had only known each other for five months before we got married. Did I tell you that? Of course I did.
Just checking!
Ah I remember it well! At least I remember my Mother throwing up her hands and yelling 'NO!'
But sorry, er yes! What the hell was I thinking? I hardly knew this man. He threw TVs at people for Gods sake! Don't ask....please don't ask....oh go on then!

Long story short, his landlord told him to get out because he was behind with his rent. So like all Romany men when confronted with anger, he picked up the TV and chucked it across the room.
Like you do!
I was told that he didn't do that in normal circumstances. In fact throwing a television was probably the stupidest thing he had done for a while considering that he would normally either 'chor it (steal) or sell it on because, cough....it did belong to him! Oh yes................!
To be fair, he had been living on the streets. He had no job. And at that point he was totally pissed off with the way people were treating him.
So as you can see I met him at a rather sad and twitchy time. Which by the end of the first week had completely changed because I had come into his life.
Ah, I can hear you say! His words, not mine!

Anyway, with a spit and a shovel, as they say, we tied the knot, jumped the broom and wed on a Saturday in Maidenhead town hall.

-

18th November 1978.............

The day dawned lovely and sunny.
 No it didn't!
What did you expect? It was the middle of November!
Okay, start again!
It was a cold dark miserable day. But I didn't care. I was getting married!
After getting dressed and fussed about by my Mum and Dad and given advice that was, well, slightly over late.....such as...
'You know what happens on your wedding night don't you dear?' my Mum.
And.....
'Oh for goodness sake Ena, leave her alone she's not stupid!' my Dad.
I just smiled and said...
'Yes thanks, that's fine. I'm sure I will cope, um...!'
I closed my eyes against the pictures that were popping up in my mind.
Ah memories...........!

2 months before the wedding and...........

Me and Jake 'at it' like rabbits in the caravan which was parked at the bottom of the garden.
There were no fairies to watch us, only spiders, well one huge one that caused me to shriek blue murder, until the passion took me and I forgot about it till we had finished, then I searched the whole vardo in sheer panic.
'Where is the bloody thing? Is it in my hair?'
'No!'
'Well where is the stupid creepy thing?'
'Its on the bed.'
'What?'
'Its on the bed! Hold on, I'll grab it.' With a grunt, Jake caught it and threw it out the window.
'Was it.......?' I shuddered and shook my hair out, still not quite believing it wasn't trying to climb in my ear.
'Na, it was dangling above me 'ead, I 'ad one eye on it all the time!'
Really? All the time? Even when we were.....?

I was brought back to reality from my musings with the dulcet tones of my Mother in my other ear.
'There we go, you look really nice dear.' She frowned.
'If only it was someone else you were marrying.....!'
Thanks mum........!

The ceremony went off well.
Sort of.
My poor brother was so busy running people around in his little triumph herald that he totally missed the whole thing.
I had a huge bouquet of mixed flowers, and standing there at the altar I thought that I looked pretty special even if I say so myself!
Until I heard the sweet sounds of hubby shouting,
'Ha ha, are they plastic?' next second he was there pulling at the flowers and trying to sniff the petals.

'Gerroff! Whatcha doin'?' I grabbed the flowers and swung to my right.
'Only jokin'! Just thought I would lighten the moment!'
Jake stood there grinning from ear to ear, and all I could hear was his relatives, his Romany relatives...yelling from the back of the room......
'Go on me lad, jump that broom get 'er wed so we can go and get pissed!'
And.......

'Get 'er 'ome and make them bed springs creak!' this was followed by a howl of laughter, rude gestures and   then humble apologies at the stewed prune indignant faces of my family and friends over in the corner.

'Um sorry missus, didn't mean no dissrespect!' doffing his cap the uncle/cousin, who the hell was he? grovelled and swooped low in a bow, then humbly sat back down.

Oh lord!
 Talk about the fine line between two halves! On the one side was my family, looking all smart and royal.
 On the other was Romany Rai and the gypsy Kings!
Well as the good old gypsy saying goes, 'The dog that digs deepest finds the bones!'
I suppose that means I am the dog. Woof.

 Soon the whole thing was over.
 As we were leaving the building people stopped and stared.
There in front of us was a huge black Rolls Royce car.
'Well I never!' said Jakes uncle Jeb, 'Will ye look at that!'
 Scratching his head in amazement he watched as we, my husband and I...ha! walked slowly round to the other side. And out of sight we jumped into the car.
Then, as we pulled away there was a huge roar of laughter as we appeared from behind the Rolls Royce and drove of in a tiny little worn out red Mini cooper!
'Ha ha well done Jake!'
'Good laugh there boy, hee hee!'
And to the sounds of laughter and clapping we headed back to the pub to get ready for the reception.
Now at this point I have to say it was a great wedding. Everybody was there. On his side, Jakes mum and dad, aunts uncles, friends, cousins, second cousins, and cousins once removed.
Some not removed far enough! And others? Well lets just say never to be seen again thank goodness!
 Nuff said!
And on my side was my mum, dad, aunt, and brother. Just a few of us. But I did have loads of mates.
And one in particular!
Oh lord!
My beautiful vibrant hysterical best friend in the world, Lesley.
Whenever I think of her I get tearful as she is no longer with us.
But thinking back, some of my funniest tales always involved her. On this occasion she was in full swing as usual.
As I entered the bar I could hear whoops of laughter, and clapping. Les had arrived before me, I see!
Turning the corner I could see she was dancing in front of the open fire, a glass in one hand and a....what the hell was that?
She saw me and yelled 'Here they come, make way, make way,' as she staggered across the room.
'Congratulations!' she said kissing me and then draping round Jake.
'Lets get this partee startedddd..!' and of she went with a feather duster, yep that was the 'thing', god knows where she got it from, and her glass of wine.
I noticed that there was something floating in it.
'Les, Les!' I pushed through the crowd. 'What the heck is that in your glass?'

'Its a pickled onion!' her voice going alto, then screaming with laughter!
I grinned. Trust her!
'It seems to have gone down very well with all these lovely gorgeous handsome....!'
Yep I got the picture! Les was in her element! She loved men. We all did, but Les...?
'Eeny meeny mack aracka who's gonna be played on their maracas....!'
She was happy and so were the guys by the look of it!
The party went well. If you could call the bizarre and weird well!
I mean, lets face it. We grow up seeing our parents as, well parents. And as parents they
'never go out, never have friends and always wear green on a Wednesday!
You get my point.
But there was my mum talking to Jakes parole officer...yes I know, less said the better.
My dad was nattering full force with the vicar. Who invited the vicar?

My aunt was eating sausage rolls and chattering away with an older member of the gypsy family, an old dear who was getting louder and louder. They were both waving their arms around like two blackbirds trying to fly!

And last but not least my brother in the middle of the gypsy men chatting away as if he had grown up with them.
Weird! Did I say weird? Yep.....totally!
I started to hum 'When two worlds collide' which quickly changed to 'Who put the bomp in the.....' just as great aunt Rosie snatched the wedding cake off the table and kindly informed everybody that, 'I made that, its up ta me who tastes it!'
Leaving poor aunt Mabel, my side, looking bemused and on the point of tears.
Rushing over I grabbed four profiteroles and a doughnut off the plate rack and thrust them in her hands.
'There aunty, this is much nicer!'

All in all it was a special, strange and plainly wonderful day.
They all stood outside to watch us go off on honeymoon, waving madly after us both, and some with tears in their eyes.
The Romany side, because it was a good get together, and my mum? because I had got married and....
'She's my little girl, she's far to young for marriage!' Sob!
We headed off towards the motorway. Our honeymoon was going to be a bit, um, strange to say the least!
We had been invited down to Taunton in Somerset by friends of Jakes.
Well not exactly friends......!
  Many years before I met him, Jake had been in all sorts of trouble which culminated in him being carted off to a halfway house!
This involved living with other men at a farm run by two lovely people who made sure the inmates worked on the land, cleaned the house and generally kept out of trouble.
These paragons of virtue, and I say it with the utmost respect, were named Patty and Trevor.

They had set Jake back on the right road, and helped him stay out of trouble.
This is where we were going to spend our honeymoon!

Oh crap cakes!
Off into the unknown. Well at least it was different!

There was no good asking Jake what it was going to be like. The car journey had rendered him partially unconscious, and the rest, a blubbering wreck of a man constantly puking his guts into a bucket that I had luckily had the sense to add to my trousseau! You know what I mean. One wedding dress, garter, something old something new, and a bucket.
Oh joy!

And yes I know a trousseau also included bedding, crockery etc, but that was so old fashioned. I was just hoping that Jake had put money by to make sure we got a bed to sleep on!

Back to the bucket, I just hoped he would have a good aim!
The trouble was he didn't drink. Not usually. Evidently the idea of marriage had made him somewhat nervous so he had decided to slip a bottle of whisky into his pocket to top up the free beer that was there for all and sundry. Pity he forgot to tell me!

We made good progress in the little old car, and four hours later we arrived at our destination.
I was actually really surprised! It was gorgeous!
A huge house in the middle of farmland.
Surrounded by flowers and trees, and they even had a few geese running around squawking at everybody.
Do geese squawk? Well whatever they did, they were pretty terrifying!
As we got out of the car the door opened and a little lady with huge glasses headed out to meet us.

'Oh how lovely to see you,' she bustled towards us. 'I see you have met our bodyguards.' she pointed towards the geese.
'They'll take your leg off if you get too near!' she laughed and leaned over to shake my hand.
'Hello dear, come on in and make yourself comfortable.' she turned to Jake 'At last! You look so, er, well?'
As Jake was standing there looking like a wet weekend in Weymouth, stinking of booze and on the point of vomiting once more, I thought Patty was being very diplomatic!

We followed her into the huge hallway and headed off to the kitchen.
'Tea?'
'Yes please Mrs.....
'Its just Patty my dear. Trevor will be down shortly and he will show you to your room.'
Turning to Jake she said, 'I think you had better go and lie down for a while son.'
Jake mumbled something totally incomprehensible and disappeared through the doorway.
'He knows where to go,' she turned and poured the tea. 'In fact he's been here so many times its a wonder he doesn't move in!'
Looking around I realised just how calming the place was.

Outside the window I could see what I though were beans growing up tall sticks.
Hedgerows full of berries grew, and there were apple trees in the distant meadow.
Fruit on the vine and lettuce, peas, and beans curling up bamboo sticks amongst rows and rows of carrots.
I smiled to myself. This wasn't half bad! No, not bad at all!
Later we met up with Trevor who gave me a big hug and a welcome.
Turning to Jake, he shook his hand and commented 'I hope you're behaving yourself now young man, especially now you have got such a beautiful wife!'
Jake just smiled, squirmed a bit and said, 'Yes sir.'
That to me, showed the respect he had for Trevor.
I had never heard him say sir before.

Trevor soon showed us around. Telling us this, and pointing out that. But soon he was off to do his work. Its a huge farm so there was plenty to do.
And of course I met the 'inmates' too!
I found, to my delight, that they thought it was great that we had decided to visit for our honeymoon.
There was a party mood and every single man was so polite to me I felt like a Princess!
'Can I get you a drink Nell?'
'Let me help you across the stile,' This was in answer to my question, 'how do we collect sloe berries?'
This was the following day after our arrival. Jake said he felt much better so we decided to go for a walk and explore.

We clambered through the overgrowth in the garden, and headed towards bushes with large purple berries on them.
There were thousands of these and I had a basket to collect them in.
'What are they for? What do you make with them?'
I was full of questions. I had never done anything like this before. Not only was it fascinating but I felt right at home.
Turning to Jake I saw that he was also completely relaxed. Big time.
He knew what to do, and for a second I realised that he had been brought up to pick all sorts of fruit like this. It was in his blood. And he was in his element.
'Its for gin making Nell, Patty and Trevor have their own gin making equipment out back in the distillery room.' Tomas helped me over the stile and lead me to one of the bushes.
'Pick as many as ya can, and then follow me.'

The next couple of hours was magical. After collecting the berries we headed over to where they were preparing to make the gin.
I had never seen anything like it before. This was part of Jake that I hadn't discovered yet.
He was content. With a smile on his face he did as he was told, no arguing!
'Makes a change' I thought!
As he sat there for hours watching and helping,
I realised then just how clever Patty and Trevor were.
There wasn't any harsh rules, no do this and that. Just love and kindness.
Over the next week we played snooker to gails of laughter, drunk wine and beer and had a generally good time.

When we left I was determined to go and see them again one day.
And we did many times.
On the journey home I realised that I had discovered something about myself.
We live very narrow lives. We go to school, study, go round friends houses, then get a job.
We centre on our families and friends.
If they don't visit somewhere different then neither do we.
It was then that I realised by marrying Jake I had broadened my horizons significantly.
I just hope it was in the right way!

Soon we were back home, which at this early stage in our marriage, was sharing with the old man and his lodger.
And did I mention that I was pregnant? In fact what with all the advice from my mum and dad about 'Do you know what to do on your wedding night?' I had totally forgotten to tell them, um!
We had the caravan parked at the bottom of the garden, but the problem was where to put it.
We needed a caravan site.

Chapter 21

January 1979.......

We got in touch with the local council. Funnily enough it didn't take long for them to get back to us with a yes!
I say funnily enough because, lets face it, If we had asked for a house we would have had to wait years!

It only took a couple of weeks to receive the letter stating where to go, what number plot and so on.

White Waltham.
I wasn't sure where that was.
'Jake where the hell is White Waltham?'
He scratched his head.
'Not sure to be honest, I think its near Maidenhead.'
And indeed it was.
In fact we were to stay at Woodlands Park caravan site, which is near the famous White Waltham aerodrome.

It was soon moving day, and with a slight feeling of trepidation, we were off!
It took a while to get used to living in a trailer I can tell ya!
It seemed so small after being brought up in a large house.
But I soon got used to it. In fact I came to love that little spot in the middle of rows and rows of vans.
On the other hand, I never got used to the idea of letting my family know I was expecting!
So I chickened out and phoned my brother.
'Hiya Andy, what you doing?'
'Nothing much why what's up?'
'Um, well better just say it really. I am up the duff without a paddle!'
'You what?'
'Oh dear lord....'
'I'm pregnant you dumb-ass!'
'Oh.'
Silence.

'Hello?'
'yeah, I'm here, just taking it all in.'
'Can you tell mum for me?'
'What, you want me to tell her?'
'Yes please.' I chewed on my nail, getting more nervous by the minute.
'Yeah, okay I'll tell her, but she won't be happy!'
'Yeah I get that! Thanks Andy, speak later.'
I let out the breath I was holding and placed the phone back in its cradle.
'Well that went well! Not!' I muttered.
Turned out that actually it was fine.
After a few 'Is that why you got married?'
And..........
'Well I might have guessed! Don't ask me to babysit all the time will you? What with your dad being ill and.......!'
Yep I got it!
I loved my mum and dad but sometimes my mother could be so old fashioned. But it wasn't her fault. They had me when they were in their forties. And things were different when they were young.
Someone had to break the mould.
And guess what?
Yep it was me!

One warm summers day a year after we got married, Jake said, 'Let's go and visit my uncle Alby and aunt Janey.'
We were sitting outside the caravan on the grass. Jake was pushing around an old lawn mower which puttered and puffed like an old man as it tried to cut through the tangle of weeds and dandelions.
Jake gritted his teeth looking like he was going to throw it over the wall.

I lay on the grass at the front of the garden with my son playing on the blanket in front of me.
'How we going to get there?' I smiled as my son blew a raspberry and then promptly fell over sideways. He hadn't quite got the art of sitting up yet. At six months he was just starting to get his balance.
'I'll get Tom to give us a lift, he won't mind.' picking up the mower he shoved it underneath the caravan and stood up.

Two seconds later, he was over the fence and headed towards a big grey caravan three doors up.
'This will be interesting!' I thought as I gathered up all my stuff and picked up my son. I had never met Alby and Janey before.

Heading indoors I quickly tidied round, went to the loo and then sorted out my son for the car journey.
When Jake came back we were ready to go.
'Okay?' Jake took Dan and before I could answer, he was strapping him in the car seat.
Tom smiled and said hello. Then turned and started the engine.
And we were off!

Alby and Janey lived in Mansion Lane Colnbrook near Slough, not too far away from us.
After about half an hour Jake told Tom to slow down so that he could get his bearings.
Pointing towards a side road, Jake yelled 'Nearly there!'
He leaned out of the window as Tom turned into the lane.
Smiling, he was just about to say something when there was a loud yell and the sound of dogs barking madly.
'Oh shite!' Jake turned to Tom. 'You're in the wrong site, ours is up the road on the left! Hang on, I'll get out and talk to them!'
Turning to the window, I let out a yell!
'He's got a gun, Jake!' I started struggling with the door handle.
'Calm down,' Tom turned to me, 'Look!'
I quickly turned back and saw Jake shaking hands with one of the two men, who had run out of the caravan with a look of murder on his face!
The gun, which had been pointed at us was now being lowered.
'Alright mush, sorry, we got the wrong vardo's, its kushti.' the two dogs were sitting down, but their teeth were pulled back and they were growling.
The other guy had a hand on each collar.

Both men were huge. Wearing short sleeved cut off shirts, dirty trousers and no shoes. Over their shoulder I could see a huge square looking caravan. It was nothing like I had seen before.

It looked more like a horse box but on bricks. The windows were really high up, and the door was six steps up from the ground. Two filthy children were playing on the steps. The little girl (girl?) turned to look at us, while rooting around in her nose with a dirty finger.

The other, a boy just sat on the ground looking listless.

'Cheers mush, seeya.' Jake jumped into the car.

'Move!' he quickly clicked his seatbelt and banged his hand on the dashboard.

We shot off like the hounds of hell were after us. Leaving two irate men, and two Dobermann pincher's snarling and dribbling after us. The gun (rifle?) was now aimed at the ground.

'Bloody hell, bloody fucking.......!'

I started to shake. I was scared to death! I turned to my son, but he was sleeping in his chair.

Even Jake looked shook up, but soon he turned with a smile.

'No problem!'

'Who were they?' I squinted back at the receding caravan site, scared that they might have changed their minds and ran after us.

'They were pikies!' Jake scratched his head, and whistled through his lips.

I raised my brows and went to say something. But nothing came out. I must have been more shocked than I thought.

'Pikies?' I managed.

'Yep, Romany's that have been kicked out of the family. Mixed in with Irish travellers.' he lit a cigarette, and blew the smoke out of the window.

'What....?' I just felt totally puzzled. What the hell was going on?

'They looked filthy and really bloody terrifying, whoever they were!'

'Yeah, we were lucky! If we had been the council or something I doubt if we would have got out in one piece!'

I could believe that!

'Not all pikies, Irish travellers or anyone else are all like that, most are good sorts. But sometimes you come across the bad 'uns. And we just did!'

Jake pointed up the road.

'Ah there's us!'

Across the road on the left, we could see a caravan park coming into sight. It looked clean and tidy.

'Phew thank goodness for that!'

As we drew up, the caravan door swung open and a little lady stepped out. I had never seen anyone looking so 'gypsy' before!

She was the epitome of a Romany woman.

Small, thin, and a ruddy complexion but with apple cheeks and dark eyes.

Her black hair was in two plaits and she had huge gold hoops in her ears. Her teeth were sparkling white and she wore a knee length pleated skirt with a snow white apron over

the front. Her blouse was full of frills and this was all topped off with a huge broach at her neck.
I was enchanted.
At this point I expect you're all thinking;
What an idiot! Gypsies are just normal people blah, blah.
Yes I know! I don't need you lot yelling at me with that look on your face.
But what you have to understand is that this little lady was what I expected gypsies to look like.
Not the bad press which we constantly have to listen to these days.
Aunt Janey was a Gypsy. And it was so cool.
You have got to understand that for a gorgi like me, the only gypsies I had ever seen were on fairgrounds or around the site.
This one was family.

'Come on in young Jake, and bring the luvverly lady and chavi with ya.' she stepped back inside, so we scrambled out of the car and followed her up the steps.
I looked around, not knowing what to expect. And I wasn't disappointed.
The caravan was like a palace! One of the first things I noticed was a beautiful old Welsh dresser covered in plates and cups. Leaning closer I could see the gold rim on the cups, and the patterns that were so intricate.

Further into the vardo we noticed pure white leather upholstery, a small glass coffee table and delicately stitched antimacassars on the back of the chairs.
From the outside of the caravan you would never have guessed just how spectacular it really was.

Not only was it spotless, I was afraid to step on the thick pile beige carpet that ran through the whole caravan.
Then I noticed sitting in the corner on the long stretch seat was an elderly man. He was wearing a trilby hat which was perched precariously on one side of his head, and a corduroy jacket with elbow patches.
All this was noticed in a few seconds. And then we were invited to sit down.

'Hiya Janey my love, how ya doin?' Jake gave her a hug then went over to the old man.
'Alby, you never change do ya?' as Jake shook his hand.
'Hello me ol' chal, how ya doin?' Alby groaned and stood up. Shaking Jake by the hand he came over and peered at me and my son.

Dan was enthralled and reached out to be picked up. His little baby hands tried to grab onto Alby's jacket.
'Ah what a lacho chavo!'
I frowned at Jake and mouthed, 'What?'
Jake mouthed back 'Good boy.'
'Ah you gives 'im to me, what a lovely young 'un.' Janey picked up Dan and headed over to the kitchen sink.
'You want a drink odjus boy?' and handed him a small beaker which she added some juice, and passed it to me to check it was okay.

Nodding, I passed it back. And Dan drank it down with gusto.
'Well palesko, what you been doing wiv yourself?' Alby asked Jake.
'Ah you know, mooching here and there, doing a bit o' metal an' that.'

I noticed that Alby talked with a lisp, and what with the gypsy accent he was hard to follow.
I've learned over the years that British gypsies have a lovely flowing sound to their voices.
Not like us with our many accents, they tend to skip over the words rather like someone skimming stones over water.
Its the only way to describe it. Irish Travellers have the same intonation. Only their's are mixed in with the wonderful Irish brogue.
   Soon I noticed something that was really familiar.
Ever since I had married Jake we seem to have accumulated hundreds of china ornaments!
They were everywhere. In our caravan we had them on the window sill, by the sink, in the bedroom. There was even a china goose in the toilet!
And here it was the same.
Janey had a taste for bone china tea sets. But also dotted around, were various statuettes of people, dogs cats and hares.

It was the same when we went to visit Jakes grandmother in her caravan. I remember seeing a small coffee table smothered in figurines. I thought 'How on earth does she keep them clean?'

Of course everything was totally polished and spotless. Puts my cleaning skills to shame!

   Soon I was brought back to the present with Janey presenting us with a huge tray laden with cakes, biscuits and a pot of tea.
   'Luvvy pot o' char,' Alby lisped over his cup.
Putting it down he sat back and started twiddling his thumbs. At least you got some scran in today!'
'Now don't you's start...!' Janey started laughing.
'You can laugh woman! Soup, tell 'em about the soup!'
Alby frowned, trying not to smile.
'Okay, I'll tells em then!'

Shifting on his chair, he settled into place.
'I was starving the other day, starving I was. And she,' he said pointing to Janey, 'said she 'ad loads of food in the cupboards!'
'Well I did Alby.....!' Janey piped in.
She leaned on the counter, enjoying the story.
'Yeah, an' what was it then? Soup!'
Scratching his head, and looking bemused he carried on.
'Soup, chicken soup, tomater soup, muliger toowny soup, and last but not least......' he stopped. And we all yelled together, 'MUSHROOM SOUP!'
We nearly fell over laughing!

Alby laughed. He snorted, he guffawed. 'What sorta woman does that ta yer?' then he laughed again.
Reaching over, he took his pipe from his top pocket, reached down and picked up the baccy bag.
We watched as he squashed it down in the pan and lit it with a match. The flame burned bright then dimmed as he inhaled. Throwing the match into the ashtray he
took a deep breath and leaned back. His eyes turned to the window, memories shone from his face.

'You's remember ol' Plato do you Jakey?'
Jake nodded and took a bite of his biscuit.
'Well he had some tales t' tell, did'nt 'e Janey?'
I noticed the lisp got more pronounced the more he got into the tale.
'He was me simensa, I really miss him these days,' he reached down between the chair legs and grabbed an old photograph album. 'Not many people had a cousin like 'im.'
Over tea and cakes we learned all about Plato. The wandering rag and bone man.
He was a character by all sounds.

'His horse and cart was his life. Collecting anything from rags to scrap metal. He would scramble over the top of sheds, down hills and all the time yelling "O 'O come on there grai's, as he trotted along.'
Alby sighed.
Janey leaned forward and touched him on his arm.
'But you remember the ol' goldfish 'e had in the wagon dontcha?'

At this, Alby started to laugh. By this time he was eating a biscuit, and most of it got caught between his lisp and his hiccuping cackle.
I was just about to reach across to get him a tissue, when Janey, with the art of forty years practice, stepped up close and wiped his face with her apron.
Ah, that's what its there for!

When he got his breath back he carried on with the story.
His shoulders still upping and downing with laughter, he said;
'Ever time 'e got a kushti deal, 'e gave 'em a goldfish!'
and of he went again. Laughing so hard he had to wipe the tears from his eyes.

'The look on them gorgi faces was a treat.' he mimed handing out a gold fish.
"Ere yar love, have a fish for ya trouble!' he sat back and his eyes crinkled with laughter.

"E loved that ol' 'ouse out on ter moor, didn't 'e?'
Janey smiled and refilled his cup.
'Ay he did that, what a character 'e was.' Stirring her cup she went on, 'Do you know? 'e used to get 5 shillings and sixpence for those rags, good vonga in them day's.'

I looked at Jake. He was absorbed in the story. His eyes lit up with memory.

I gently stood up, and picking up my son, headed out the door. He needed feeding, and I felt that I was intruding in some long forgotten reminiscence that had nothing to do with my world.

They never noticed me slip away, and I was grateful. I didn't want to put them out. Outside was a different picture. Some caravans, I could see, were in need of repair, and others were brand new. Sitting down on the step I gave my son his bottle, and gently rocked him.
I felt a presence and looking up, saw a young boy peering over the fence.
I smiled. He smiled back and ran on to play with his friend who was sitting in the garden of the van at the corner of the road.

These people were alright. In fact I don't think I had ever met such lovely warm families. It seemed to me that some cultures are maligned because they are unfamiliar. What people don't understand, they don't like.
It was so unfair.
I don't know how long I sat there, but all of a sudden the door opened and Janey popped her head out.
'Alright lovey?' she smiled.
'Yes thank you, just feeding my boy.' handing him to her, I clambered to my feet and started up the steps.
Janey was looking down at Dan, and the warmth in her eyes said it all.
We went back inside and finished off the tea. Soon It was time to leave.
'don' leave it too long nex' time, ya hear?' said Alby.
We left them on the steps, two lovely warm people with hearts of gold.
I didn't realise that would be the only time I would ever see them. We never seemed to head that way again after that.
   As the years went by we got to see Jakes Gran and Granddad, but Alby and Janey faded into the past.

   Jakes step Grandad, on the other hand, was a real character.
Gina and Jacko lived on a caravan site in Maidenhead.
They had a mobile home or double trailer, with a garden and shed.
Gina was a lovely lady. She couldn't read or write like a lot of traveller women so every time we went for a visit she would hand me copious amounts of letters to read to her. Some of them were months old.
'What if these were really important bills?' I asked her one day.
'Ah never mind them bills, they get paid if someone comes a'knockin' on me door!'
Fair enough!

Jacko on the other hand was a miserable old sod! But funny with it!
The amount of times we turned up for a cuppa and he would say; 'What you doing 'ere? Can't you use that phone thing 'efore you get 'ere?'
'Ah leave 'em alone Jacky, they's come to see me!'
Gina would invite us in, make tea and sit us down. It was only when we were settled on the settee would she ask what was going on in the world.
Or more to the point get Jake to do something for her, leaving me with Jacko!

And he never said a lot to be honest. But me being me I felt like I had to make conversation.

One day when we had been there for about an hour I couldn't stand the silence any longer.

'Erm, so.....' I said twisting my fingers into a knot, 'how have you been?'

His rheumy eyes swivelled my way and he grunted.

'Erm, yes.' Was the answer.

Okay start again,' I felt myself fiddling with my shirt, so I took my hand away and sat on it.

'Would you like me to cut some cake for you?'

Shifting slightly in his chair, he stared at the cake.

'No, no I can do that, I loves me football cake!'

Football cake? What the......

'Anyway..' Jake strolled back into the room, 'I'll get that fixed for you.'

Turning to Jacko, 'Hello Jacko, how ya doin'?'

'How many more peoples gonna ask me that?' he got up and stomped around the room.

Flinging open a window he breathed in a great gulp of fresh air before blowing it out. I think he hoped we would go with it!

He picked up an ornament, put it down.

Moved a tin, slid it across the table and then put that down too.

Jake winked at me.

'Got any more pants and vesties Jacko?'

'You being funny young Jake?'

'No, course not!' Jake looked the picture of innocence.

I tried not to smile.

This was typical banter between the two of them.

Jacko was typical of the older Romany men.

He wore a trilby on his head like Alby, and an old cardigan over baggy trousers.

Gina was very much like her sister Janey. She had short black hair, swarthy skin and twinkling eyes. She was the serious sister. She never said a lot, but would always treat you with respect.

'You goin' down the town Gina?' Jacko squinted at her.

'Why?' Gina peered at him over her glasses.

'Cos I need anovver fly cake and some of them hot nobs!'

'Fly cake and.....what?!' eyes wide I looked to Jake.

He was killing himself laughing. He mouthed to me,

'Told ya!'

And indeed he did! Before we got there, he had told me; 'Watch out for Jacko and his football cake and fly cake. His hot nobs are another one!'

Grinning from ear to ear he just looked at me.

I didn't ask.

By this time I was used to the weird and wonderful world of gypsy language.

And that's just the English version!

We stayed a few hours then left with promises of return visits. Carrying cakes, biscuits and those hot nobs! (hob nobs, well what did you think I meant?!)

Hot nobs. Yep, sounds good to me!

Chapter 22

The one thing that puzzled me, but also left me smiling, was the gypsy way of story telling.
Their tales were wonderful.
But it was the real life stories with a touch of gypsy sparkle and twist that always amazed and amused me!
I called it the 'let's fill in the gaps with treacle' stories. They were so colourful and dramatic.

For example, 'You's don't put that on yer teeth dinlo, it will make them turn red and fall out!
Or....
My ol' paridala (grandmother) used to tell us tha' if you wash yer face in pani from a clean spring you'll tek thems wrinkles and throw em away!'
Of course it didn't end there.
The conversation would be followed by all the elders in the family nodding their heads and shifting in their seats. One or two would wave their arms and gesture towards the old lady sitting in the corner, mouth open to flies, snoring gently.
'You's only got to look at our ol' Rosie, she's an 'undred and ten, no wrinkles, see?'
With a sniff the other old lady would reach over and grab a biscuit. Then carry on from where they had left off.
'I remember's seein' her riding that ol' bike when I was a nipper, she must a' been 80 then!'
With that, they would nod their head in confirmation.
The others would sigh, the air shifting slightly in the breeze of their astonishment.
If I was party to their talk, I would keep my mouth shut and just drink it all in.
I learned long ago that reality, dreams and imagination are a huge part of gypsy culture. And lets face it, maybe they are right. I mean, who's to say that what they believe is wrong?

I smiled when I heard this one.
'Our Jim, he's just bought 'imself a huge ol' vardo, it belonged to the king o' the gypsies!'
This was met with a huge intake of breath, then chattering commenced in a wave of sound.
A mixture of birds and gravel.

'Tell us about da chavi then, what he buy? Where he get it then?'
'Ah ol' Timmo down the road in in Devon.'
At this point I have to add that most gypsies don't set much store to time or distance. Say you lived in London? They would be in Cumbria, but to them it was 'five minutes darn the road!'

If it was 10 o clock, and they needed to meet up at 12, you can guarantee they would be late.
And so on.
So colourful, fun and different. I loved listening in to their stories. Told with much hugging, tutting and laughing raucously at the men who would always think they were right in every way.
The men took themselves so seriously, the women, on the other hand took it all with a huge pinch of salt!
   The gypsy character and culture is still going strong, but modern life hasn't been kind to them.
   New caravans do not have that psychological effect of romantisism that the old time vardo's had.
   To see a shiny brand new van appear on private land turns the mildest of people into a raging wolf.
   Hard times on the road and the continuous harassment from local councils do nothing for the gypsy's esteem.
   Back in the day people were much more tolerant. In fact the idea of seeing the old gypsy wagons rolling into the village was a cause for excitement.
You knew that the next few days would be amazing.

   Children would sneak out of their house at night to watch the gypsy's dance and hear the music being played. So much more exotic than their everyday life. The colour of the vardo's, the handsome young men and the pretty women.
It bubbled up inside like fizzy pop.
The Gypsies were in Town, Yeah!

Not any more. I don't know what's happened. Its so sad.
Poverty greed and 'all about me' syndrome is strong around the world these days. But back in the early eighties it was still there. Blue sky, red dresses, gold earrings and laughter.
And if you are lucky enough to know these amazing people, then you know that you are part of something rather special.
   Sitting on the step watching chubby arms dipping into the puddles, peals of laughter as the kids had fun, made it all worth while. Yes they may have looked grubby or dirty, but it was clean fun and hard work.

That I believe, is the crux of the matter. Most modern folk don't believe that gypsies are hard workers.
But trust me, they are!
Who else would push a cart with one woman, a child and a huge bag of metal two miles to the scrap yard?

Most people just get in their huge four by fours and head off to the office.
Not a gypsie. They graft. Roads, roofs, gardens and scrap. Wheeling and dealing. No more trouble makers than a lot of gorgi's.
Unless of course you could count that water barrel and copper tank I mentioned before! (cough!)

Chapter 23

But that does take me to another warm sunny day. White clouds skidding across the sky, bees a'buzzing in the yard and a huge rat hiding under my bed!

You just knew it was going to be one of those days! And Jake was centre stage! (Oh surprise!)

I will never forget it. As long as I live and breath. I can see it now in full technicolour. And believe me when I say that I will never let them forget it either!
There I was, round Belles, having a lovely cup of tea thinking to myself, 'well this is a bit more civilised after the whoo ha with the Indian costume, a bloody nose and an embarrassed husband.'

I should have kept my big mouth shut.
All of a sudden there was a bang on the caravan door.
And..........................
'Who's that?' Yelled Belle.
'Me,' said Jake 'Have you got a hammer?'
What now, I thought. *Here we go......!*
'Its in the shed,' Belle got up and opened the door. 'What's up?'

'Its a bloody great rat, its got in me caravan, and we can't catch it!'
Jake rushed in, rushed out, and headed straight back to our caravan.
'Oh great, now we got to go and catch a rat!' I mumbled.
Holding open the door, I yelled over my shoulder.
'Coming?'
Laughing, Belle replied; 'Ooh I wouldn't miss this for the world.'
Walking over to the van I yelled 'Where are you?' I stuck my head round the door.
'In here.' Came Jakes muffled voice.
'They're in the bedroom. Great now the rats going to get into my bed.'
'Won't be the first time I had a rat in my bed!' Belle giggled.
I started to laugh, and by the time we got to the bedroom we were both hysterical.
But that was nothing compared to the scene in front of us!

Two grown Gypsy men, hard as nails, who could eat you for breakfast if you looked at them the wrong way, were standing on the bed.
My bed!
Clutching each other so they wouldn't fall arse over tit. One of them, Jake I think, yelled; 'Where is it? Where's the bloody scabby dirty thing gone?'
Then.....
'You get it!'
'No, you go get it, its your van!'
Belle and I just stared.
Before we had a chance to yell 'You bloody cowards!' A movement caught my eye.
In the middle of the floor was the cutest little bundle imaginable.
It was a field mouse! A tiny bloody field mouse!
With big eyes, and little paws.
It was shivering.
Scared out of its wits because two hulking great men where screaming at it!
I bent down and scooped it up.
'Come on little guy, I won't let those nasty men get you!'
Holding the little cutie pie to my chest, I glared at the guys and headed out the door, with Belle exclaiming, 'Aw isn't it gorgeous?'

We never said anything as we let the little mouse go. As we watched it scurry away, she turned to me and said, 'I think we need a drink, shall we go to the pub and let them babysit? You never know we might find ourselves some real men!'
Yep gypsy men can be scared of stuff! Who knew?

But joking apart traveller and gypsy men are hard. Mentally and physically.
I may have laughed at Jake and Tim going on about a mouse but I knew, and so did Belle, that they were acting silly. Just trying to make us laugh.

Its easy to get complacent when you live with a gypsy man. He may come across as soft, or sweet, but get him in a situation when it drives the blood up and you'll see a change come over him.

I learned that lesson a few years ago when I was walking home from the pub with a man friend. He made the mistake of putting his arms around me just as Jake came round the corner.

I never saw a man fly through the air so fast in all my life! He was lucky. He missed the shop window by about ten inches. And his eye was black for a week.
I yelled a bit, but Jake just looked at me and said; 'Home, now!'

Jake didn't speak to me for a few days. It wasn't until I had explained the circumstances that he then turned round and said; 'Yeah, well you'll know better in future, aye?'
Yep, I would!

Gypsy men are traditionalists. However modern they may seem, there is always that spark of 'old fashioned' about them.
Their vardo's have changed into modern caravans. Some of the women go out to work. But they stay the same as they were in the past, only with a more open mind.

Talking of tradition, one of the biggest gatherings of gypsies and travellers is on the 8th to the 14th of June every year.
Its called Appleby horse fair. Gypsies travel from all over the country to meet up in this small Cumbrian town.
Over 10,000 gypsies and travellers attend the horse fair, but at least 30,000 people turn up to take a look, watch the races and take a look at the horses.
A lot of buying and selling goes on. Horses pass from one owner to the new.
Lots of stalls selling pots and pans, and people just laughing and chatting.
Passing on news, and match making their kids. Many a gypsy or traveller has come away at the end of the Fair engaged to be married.

There's quite a bit of difference between the traditions of gypsies and Irish travellers.
For starters, Romany's don't do 'Grabbing' like the Irish.
So what's grabbing?
Until they are engaged, traveller girls are subjected to 'grabbing' by the teenage boys. Its a strange ritual, and not something Romany Gypsies do.
A boy will spot a girl that he likes, and make a grab at her to steal a kiss. The rules state that the girls are not allowed to approach the boys but the males have a free run.
But it has a darker side. The guys do their best to get the girl away from their friends, and if the girl isn't to eager, the boy is allowed to pressure her by twisting her arm, literally!
Its just a way of getting the girls phone number!

The Romany Gypsy's on the other hand, will usually meet and marry a girl within the extended family or friends.
Back in the old days when Gypsies travelled around, they would meet up at certain stops along the road, and introduce their young ladies to the suitable men.
But there were restrictions. A girl or guy could marry a gorgie, but they would expect the outsider to become one of 'us'. This is what happened to me.

After moving into the caravan and a few weeks after getting married, I was inundated with lots of visitors coming to pay their respects, and giving me and Jake lots of presents or gifts.
'I brought ya some mekk up, and crockery.' said one older lady, with a smile on her face.
Another would hand me home made cakes that were totally delicious.
When I started to protest saying 'I can't accept all these its too much, but thank you.'
I was greeted with a look of astonishment!
'O' course yez gotta tekk it!' One young woman puffed indignantly.
'You's one of us now, so this is how we greet ya!'
and with that another family member handed me a huge pile of curtains.
And they were beautiful! The stitching was so delicate, and the colours so bright.
They would look fantastic in my new caravan.

Over the years Romany courtship has become more open. Men and women choose their own mates. But parents do have a say if they believe their daughter is making the wrong choice.

The one thing that tradition still stands by is that Romany girls must keep their virginity until their marriage night.
The idea of sex before the wedding is frowned on big time!
A girl must be pure. Its a big thing for a girl to become a woman. Some Romany 'tribe's' or cultures see it as a sort of defilement that a woman must put up with until its her time to get ready to be a mother.
From a Gorgi's point of view this is very archaic, but for a Romany its a must.

All I can say is that I am glad I was a gorgi at that point because nobody told me that!
Door shut after horses bolted! (oops!)

So what did my parents think of all this romantic gypsy lifestyle?
Well as I mentioned before, they weren't that happy to start with.
My dad, bless him, took to Jake like a duck to water. After being in the army for six years or so my dad had seen the worlds worst, and the best, of men.
As he said a while later, 'There are smart men who are evil, and scruffy ones that have a heart of gold, I'm just waiting to see which one he is,' he added, 'and for his sake, Jake had better be one of the good ones!'
Thanks dad.

My mum on the other hand wasn't quite so, well, sensitive.
'Why on earth did you pick someone so...' wringing her hands and pursing her mouth...oh yeah she had that mud look on her face full force....
'He is horrible simple as that!'
She stopped in her tracks and glared at me.
Um was this a good time to tell her I was pregnant? No, thought not!
'But mum, you can't possibly tell what he's like, we've only been together a few months!'
The glare became a suspicious frown.
'So why don't you tell me what he is like?'

And she folded her arms and waited.
'Er, well, for starters....he looks after me, and.....'
'Well I should hope he damn well does!' followed by an humph, and a sniff.
'And he's a hard worker!' my fingers were crossed behind my back, and with an innocent look on my face I went on, 'In fact he's just got another job!'

'Oh yes? Doing what? Scrap metal and rags I expect!' this was said with another sniff.
I was seriously thinking about getting her a tissue when she started on her rhetoric about her time in World war 2, serving as a Sergeant in the W.A.A.F's
and stationed at North Weald.
Half way through her rant, I coughed and butted in with...
'But I thought we fought for freedom, and it was you who always stuck up for the foreigners and....'
'Yes but you are my little girl, I wanted you to marry......'
'Yes you wanted me to marry the guy up the road, and be happy with that....'
'Yes, but I never imagined.....'
And so it went on.
But the funny thing was, as time always dampens the edge of arguments, she actually became fond of Jake.

I think the turning point was when she arrived at my door. By this time I was living round that corner, in a house just five minutes away.
This particular day she was in a right state......
'What's up?' I ran to the door.
'Its Jerry, he's dead! Can Jake come and bury him for me?' she was in tears.
Now at this point I have to point out that Jerry was a cat. We are not in the habit of killing neighbours or family members and burying them in the garden.
Well not yet. If Jake keeps annoying me there is always a first time!
Anyway, back to the cat......!
'Jake? Jake! Where are you?' I ran up the stairs.
'The cats died, and mums downstairs and wants to know if you'll go round and bury it for her?'
Jake just looked at me.
'Yup, give me a spade, I'll sort it.' and standing up, he went downstairs where my mum was waiting.
Seeing her in such a state, he put his arms around her and said, 'Its alright, I'll come and do it now, come on.' and taking her by the arm he shushed her out the door.
The look on her face spoke volumes.
After that incident, they were the best of friends.
Gold star to Jake, bless him!

Getting back to the subject of being pregnant, I wasn't in any mood just after the wedding to tell my family that I was expecting.
So I bottled it. Big time. And phoned my brother, told him, then spoke to my aunt. She kindly told me that she would pass on the message but added....
'You do know what your mother will say, don't you?'
silence down the phone.

'Um, what?' I grimaced at the phone, trying to hold it as far away as possible from my ear. I knew it was stupid, but it made me feel less, well, naked!
'I think you know.' said my aunt primly.

'Oh yeah.' I thought. I could imagine.
'You only married him because you were expecting!'
And.........
'You could have come home and had the baby, we wouldn't mind just as long as you get away from him! I rue the day you went to work in Maidenhead!'

Of course, this was long before the cat incident.
   I knew one thing from a very early stage in my relationship.
Whatever state I got in with money, or problems, I would never ask them for help.
I made my bed, and I would lie in it. Albeit whether it had covers on or old coats! Long story......!

Chapter 24

   Which takes me to the time that sticks out in my mind.
The months of hardship. I had never been without before. Its not something you think about until its there in your face. We were broke. Stony broke.
We'd been living in the vardo for a few months and the money had dried up. Big time.

   There was no work, and having to go on social security was not only embarrassing but the amount they gave you to live on was pittance.
I knew we had to do something but what?
I eventually found a cleaning job, and Jake threw his hand in with one of the other mushes doing scrap metal.
But it taught me one lesson. Never rely on family for handouts, and just because I was brought up with enough vonga, doesn't mean that one day it won't run out!

   My mum and dad were never well off, but we always had enough you know? But I'd thrown myself into this mysterious strange world, so I would have to learn their ways or fail.
Then one day Jake fell ill. He had contracted septicaemia, which is a form of blood poisoning. It was caused by all the dirty metal that he handled.
He must have cut himself without realising it.
What a nightmare!
He was taken into hospital where he was on a drip and antibiotics for two weeks. When he came home he was exhausted. And we were still broke.

Our son was still very small, I was handling two cleaning jobs and trying to keep the caravan going at the same time.

Life with a gypsy is a bit like a precipice, you teeter on the edge most of the time, but one push and you fall off. Big time.
But I still would not ask my family for help. It was a matter of principal.
I learned something that day. You are on your own.
You may have others around you but its up to you to stop being a dinlo and balls up!

Being a gypsy can be a hard life. Each can hold their own, but if you need help you'll get it. But you have to pay it back, not necessarily in kind.
A favour, money or even 'seeing to someone' is more common.
Luckily we didn't have to do the third!
We got through it, and I soon got the hang of their ways.
No one was going to pogger us!

Talking of trying to break us, it was the gorgi's on the site that drove us to distraction.
And that's the funny thing.
You would think that gypsies would be at each others throats every five minutes. But on the whole they get on pretty well.
The good thing about them is if they have an argument or grudge, its there, out in the open. A couple of fights, a broken nose then its over, and then back to normal.

Most times the shora, or elder would get the two together and make them either shake hands or fight. There wasn't much call for a shora on a modern caravan site, but somehow they always had one older man who seemed to take on this role, whether he wanted it or not.
Memory and culture can't be shaken off that easily just because you live in a modern world.
On the other hand, the gorgi's were a pain in the arse!

Living all my life as a gorgi, it never dawned on me just how spiteful, cruel, bitchy or just downright childish and nasty 'normal' people can be!
Till one day when......
'Oy!'
'What?' I turned round just as I was heading indoors. Standing on the top step I leaned over the railings and saw a dumpy looking girl, typical chav type, with her arms crossed, glaring at me.
I didn't recognise her at this point because she had pissed me off just by yelling 'Oy!'
But soon her chubby miserable looking face started to filter through.
Now, I don't know if you agree, but even if someone sounds pissed off, you still smile at them till you know what's what!
In fact my favourite saying was from a film, can't remember what it was called. But in the film the older woman says to the younger, 'You are going to make a great assassin! Just remember, always smile even if its a second before you pull the trigger!'
Oh yeah, I go by that, big time!
Anyway..........

'Hello, can I help you?' I smiled indulgently. These chavs just don't understand sarcasm.....!

'Yeah you!' she shrugged her shoulders...were they shoulders? Just looked like a huge lump of lard to me, but......
'Is that your bloody great car parked in me drive? 'Ow the hell can I get me fucking mini out o' there with your fucking...' (she said fucking as though she already had a dick up her arse....) '.....great monster shit car there!'
With this she shook her flab like a washerwoman shaking a duvet, and settled two chubby hands on her waist, with a look of 'Now ya know it!' on her face.
'Come on,' said her snarl, 'let me smack ya....!'
Oh boy, she didn't know me very well did she?!
I walked slowly down the steps. The smile plastered on my face. Walking through the garden I opened the gate and stepped into the road.
She didn't expect that. Her face changed from snarl to uncertain.
Leaning closer and closer......(I set great store by peoples personal space, I was loving this....!}
I got nose to nose with her and......
'You ever talk to me like that again little girl..'(snarl, see I can do it too!) ' and I will stick that car right up your.......'
She stepped back.
'No need fer getting arsy! I only asked!' she breathed in, and a look of indignation came over her face as she stared at me.
'That is not my car.' I went on, 'and if it was I wouldn't move it now, after you talking to me like that!'
'Well I was only asking......'
'No you weren't. You were trying to scare me. Which, lets face it, is laughable! Considering......' the look on her face was priceless.......
'Considering' I went on, 'that you look like Humpty bleeding Dumpty with all that fat flapping around!'

(Yeah I know what you are thinking. I thought you said you hated bitchiness? Well I do. Unless its me using it! I'm a gorgi, get over it!')

Well the result was fascinating!
She went bright red in the face, welled up like a leaking pipe and let rip with all the obscenities should could think off!
'You bloody fucking bitch shit face.....!'
I just stood there, a look of amusement on my face.
Eventually she stopped and looked at me. Her mouth was still opening and closing like a fish without oxygen.
'Finished?' I said.
I moved closer. 'Go home, learn to speak to people with respect, and.......' with this I turned away and opened the gate, 'Just remember, the next time you speak to me like that you'll see what I learned from the Romany's!' I walked up the steps and went indoors.

Out of the window I could see her spluttering and spitting like spilt water on a hob. A big fat hob! Yes I know, bitchy, blah blah!

When I got indoors, Jake looked up from what he was doing, and said. 'Nice one, didn't need me then?' he crooked an eyebrow, lips twitching, 'I think you sorted her out. One question?'

Puzzled, I said 'what?'

'Well,' he smiled, 'I just wanted to know what it is that you learned from the Romany's?' and laughed.

'You keep on you'll find out!' laughing, I picked up a cushion and lobbed it at him!

I never did see her again.
Well I say that..... I did see her once more as she left her caravan one day. But she saw me and rushed back inside.
Can't think why, can you?!

Chapter 25

Oh those Gypsy days!
Hot sun, barbecues, screaming babies, mothers yelling 'get the fuck indoors ya mouthy little ...!' and the men sitting on the step whittling wood into small carved creatures for their chavi's.
The kids running around, snotty noses wiped on sleeves, laughing and jumping in puddles.
Old men chatting and guffawing, their laughter drifting across the garden and to our ears. Some digging and planting, others just standing around giving orders about peas and daffodils.

'Ere you gotta put that one over there, too much sun 'ere will mekk it too dry.'
'Na, I knows what I is doin' wiv it, I be plantin' those for years.'
A scratch of the head, a cluck of the tongue and off they would go again.

'Well I sees that old branch there,' one said as he leaned over and grabbed the tree. 'needs tekkin down and thrown on the yog.' shaking his head he pulled the branch down and chopped it off.

Soon the smell of woodsmoke drifted over the caravans, ah glorious!
And I could hear birds singing as I sat in my deck chair contemplating the world.
I knew that we would have to move very soon. And the idea wasn't a pleasant one.
I had lived in a house all my life, but after living in a caravan for years it was hard to think we would have to leave it again.
My son was getting older. He would soon need a room of his own.
And the caravan was beginning to fall to pieces. It was never that sturdy in the first place.
Damp patches had started to appear in the kitchen and the bedroom was never that warm.
When we bought it I thought that this time we would be here for good. But caravans don't last that long.

After the scare with my baby having whooping cough it was only sensible to get out and into a warm dry house. But after the last time I was not looking forward to it.
The idea of being a house dweller again left me with a sinking feeling.
I had basked in the warmth of a Romany glow. The friendships I had made, the company that made us feel safe, was coming to an end.
Soon we would be back with the gorgi's again!
And I hated the thought.
It felt like I was being exposed to school bullies.
I hated the thought of being out there with 'normal' people. I now knew what they could be like.

Oh I know. Not all gorgi's were nasty. Most, like my family, were respectable kind loving people.
But I also knew what the council was like.
Take a gypsy out of a caravan and put them in a decent area? Yeah, how laughable is that?

And so the day soon arrived. We had been offered a place in High Wycombe. A brand new area just been built!
Well who would have thought it?

Saying goodbye was difficult. Really hard.
'Bye then, you tekk care out there!'
'Seeya soon, dontcha be a stranger now ya hear? Don't forget us cos you are living with them gorgies avri.'
Yes 'out there' said it all.
We were going to be out there. In the world without our friends.
Old Vic came over and gave us a hug. He smelled of tobacco and woodsmoke.
I felt a sob catch in my throat.
'You's look after the chavi now ye hear?' he said rubbing Dan's head.
He put his hand in his pocket, rummaged around for a second then took it out. In it was a shiny new 50 pence piece.

Placing it in my hand he said 'That's for the boy, start up his savin' box.' he sniffed.
I leaned over and gave him a hug.
'Gonna miss you.' I kissed his cheek.

The van was ready to take us and our belongings.
There was no more time.
We all clambered in and started off down the road.
As the site began to disappear I felt a deep sadness, but also excitement.

I remember that first day turning the corner and realising that at last we had a real bona fida house!
This time it would be different. This time I would not go running back to the site. I could handle gorgies, I knew I could.
Fingers crossed, I got out of the car.
The good thing about it was the fact that we were all moving in together on the same day!
Vans were pulled up outside each of each block, and people and dogs were spilling out onto the pavement.
There were shouts of recognition between families, laughter and kids playing in the street.
Maybe this wasn't going to be as bad as I first thought.

At first it was a hive of friendliness, laughter and fun. We all borrowed bits and pieces from each other, helped with moving in and knocking up shelves.
I started to relax. Maybe this was going to be really good. A huge house, nice neighbours and just a quick jog to the shops.

But of course it didn't happen that way. The trouble was, we had got into our gypsy ways.
We started inviting people in, having a few get together's and so on.
 But these people weren't gypsies. And soon the gorgi bitchiness started.
Our next door neighbour for one.
The layout of the flats was that we all had to share a main entrance. To the left right front and side were doors to seperate apartments.
In other words, we were living on top of each other.
And that couldn't be good.
We were on the left side of the hallway, the annoying neighbour was directly to our left. Facing the main door.
And boy did she like to party! If she didn't have one guy in there with her, she had ten!
And she thought she was Gods gift!
Now at this point you have to understand something.

I had lived my marriage so far on a site where gypsies had respect for each other.
 They didn't flirt with their neighbours wives or husbands. It wasn't the done thing.
But now I was back out in the world full of trouble makers, marriage wreckers and downright bitches.
I had to learn, and learn quick!

If one girl tried getting round my old man then at least a dozen tried it. Its not that he was all that handsome, but he was, well, a gypsy!
Dark hair, dusky skin and the charm.
And did those girls try it on! I remember watching out the window one day when a young girl taking her dog for a walk came across Jake mending his bike. Flirt? Its a wonder she didn't take of her knickers and throw them at him.
I watched.
Jake smiled politely, spoke to her for a while, picked up his bike and came indoors.
By this time I was fuming! Smoke was coming out of my ears!
'So, nice was she?'
'Who?' Jake looked totally puzzled.
'The ol' tart out there trying to get your kit off!' I glared at him.
The light suddenly dawned on his face, and he laughed!
He had the nerve to laugh?! Just wait till I......!
'Don't be so bloody daft woman, we were just talking.'
I raised my eyebrows in disbelief!
'Talking? What about?'
'Just this and that.' Jake began to look uncomfortable.
'What did I do wrong?'
I sighed and patted the cushion next to me.
He sat down.
'Jake, you got to understand something,' I shifted, and looked at him. 'these girls are not like the travellers girls. These are modern women who go out with tons of guys and have no qualms in stealing another woman's husband!'

To give him credit it, he looked stunned!
'What ya mean, she was chatting me up like?'
His face was a picture.
'Yes you dumbass!' I sniffed.
His face lit up like the sunlight on the ocean.
'Well who knew? A rackli chatted me up!'
I glared. Big time.
'Yeah and don't you get used to it! Next time I'll....'
'You'll what? Smack em one?' he started laughing.
'Too bloody right I will.'
I muttered under my breath and stomped over to the window.
That was the first time it happened. But it wasn't the last.
Over the next few years I had to warn off a number of 'wannabee's' who tried it on.
To give Jake credit, he wasn't the slightest interested in them. His attitude was that if they couldn't keep to one man, then he wasn't going to be on their list of conquests.
I missed our old caravan and wanted desperately to be back in our cosy lane.
What I didn't realise was how innocent Jake was where women were concerned. He honestly believed when he was talking to a girl about tires, scrap metal and all sorts, that they were interested! Didn't dawn on him that they just wanted him!

As I said before, he wasn't much to look at but there was something about him. He had an edge. Maybe it was the Romany blood, but he attracted them like bees buzzing round a honeypot.

Pissed me off big time!

There was only one big spat we had when one woman wouldn't take no for an answer. And that was the one that I mentioned earlier. She tried putting her hand on his knee and he yelled at her so loud she nearly shot through the ceiling. Bit like that cat on Tom and Jerry!

After that she caused so much trouble. The bloody rackli hedgmumping bitch. There! I said it!

Oh the irony! We the so called high class 'normals' look down our noses at gypsies and travellers.

And yet......and yet....... ah, never mind.

Of course not all gorgi's were nasty. Just like any other race, religion or group there were good and bad.

But if there is one thing I have learned its that changing cultures isn't as easy as you would think. Finding out that the 'new' culture is better than the one you have been brought up with is pretty sobering to say the least!

Chapter 26

And so, we are here.
Two caravans, a halfway house, two more houses and finally we end up back in my town.

We were given a maisonette, which in plain English means a house on top of a flat.
I couldn't get used to it at first.
Bricks and mortar made me feel claustrophobic.
And I was wary of the the neighbours.

Living in a caravan made relationships easier. We were so close there, it was a case of getting on with each other or driving ourselves insane!

'If you's don' like that neighbour me dear, then don't bother with 'em! There's a few I like, and some I don't, but we all gets on, see. Its called respect.'
I smiled when I remembered old Tilly.
She was always giving out advice, telling people that, 'I don't like 'er, but you's can 'cos its up to you to make up yer mind!'
It was a long time ago. Poor Tilly would be dead and gone now.
I just hope she found that sparkling blue and green vardo waiting for her in the sky.
If I see a gypsy woman selling heather in the street, I will never pass by without giving her some money for a sprig, and I always take time to stop and have a chat.
I sometimes get odd looks, but it makes me smile a secret smile.
And I think to myself, I know the truth.
I know what you've been missing.
If you see a gypsy selling heather you would probably cross over to avoid her.

I on the other hand see a lovely kind hearted lady with a touching smile, grinning at me with pleasure, because I am giving her something she doesn't get very often.

A bit of respect.

But I know the secret you see, so I'll let the Gorgi's get on with their life, in ignorance of these wonderful people I had the privilege to live with.

Epilogue.

Walking over to the back door I can see trees, hedges and just a peek of the School.
To my right is an allotment, and below my balcony there are squirrel's living in the willow tree.
 High in the sky are Red Kites swirling on the thermals.
Its peaceful.
 The neighbours are friendly and now we are older. Not too old mind. I'm in my 50's and Jake is 62. Dan our son is doing well and living in Bracknell with an lovely woman.
Some gorgi's are good.

But when I close my eyes I can still see us sitting outside our vardo, Jake whistling out of tune. Me sitting on the grass playing with my baby boy.
Old Vic on his step, pipe in mouth, whittling down a wooden toy.
I can hear hammering, and I see Belle hanging out her washing, kids running in the road.
And I smell cooking coming out of the neighbours caravan window.
There's music too.
A lilting jig on a violin, a slap of feet on the ground, and the high sweet voice of a girl singing a gypsy song.
Just a memory.
 Maybe.
I smile. I think, yes I know, there's a gypsy soul in all of us. Especially me.

THE END

Nanny Gina Loveridge and her dog, Dinah. She and Jacko lived in Maidenhead, Berks.

Janey and Alby Buckland and unknown child. Jakes Uncle and Aunt who lived in Colnbrook, Slough.

The Loveridge family on holiday, mid 60's. Hayling Island. Jake is second from the left.

A recent photo of Jake with his hobby, making Gypsy Vardo's.

Dennis Loveridge. Jakes Father. Born in Bristol, but lived all his life in Maidenhead Berks.

Jake when he was young and Dan. Daniel was two years old. First time we moved into a house.

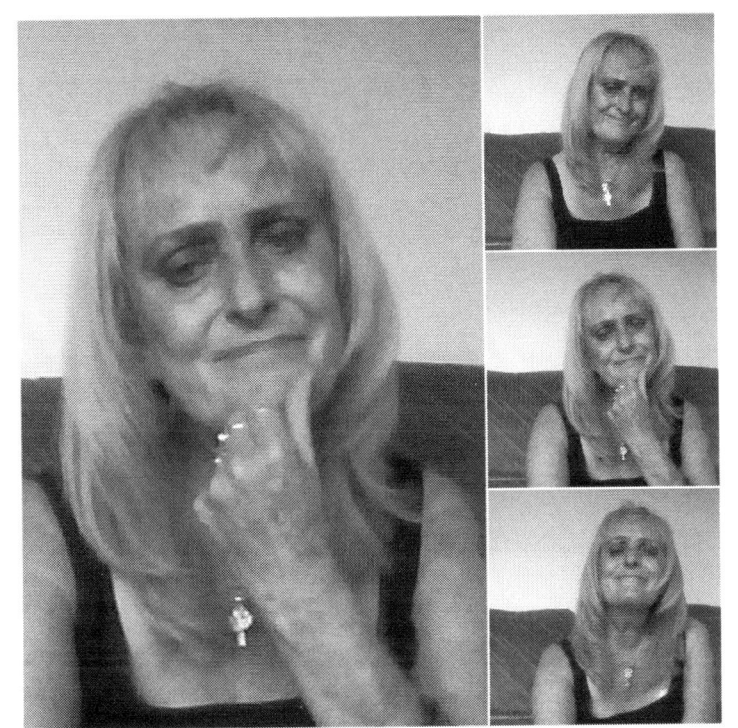

And then there's me! Nell Rose Loveridge. What can I say? Is that the end of the story? Maybe, maybe not. We will see!

And last but not least!

Jake today. Older and wiser. Well, maybe not wiser....! Still makes me laugh though!

Gypsies in History - 1931 Yarm Fair, N. Yorkshire

Gypsies and Vardo in Derby 1910.

Loveridge Family at Barnet Fair near Reading, circa 1900.

If there are any mistakes in the spelling, gypsy translations or locations, then the blame is all mine.

So much happened back then that some of the locations, and placements have had to be adjusted otherwise it would make the whole thing so complicated, and well, messy!

That's my excuse and I am sticking to it!
Nell (Melanie) Rose Loveridge. (2017)

About the Author....

Melanie (Nell) was born in Marlow Buckinghamshire England. After living on the site and various other locations, she moved back in the late 80's.

She has worked in various jobs over the years but her longest job has been in an office.
She has been writing since she was a small child.
She lives with her other half, Jake, and two goldfish, named Fish and Chips.

Printed in Poland
by Amazon Fulfillment
Poland Sp. z o.o., Wrocław